W9-BZA-011

Alexander Pushkin

# The Captain's Daughter

Illustrations
by Pavel Sokolov

*The Captain's Daughter* (also known as *The Daughter of the Commandant* or *Marie: A Story of Russian Love*) is regarded as Pushkin's best prose work. It was first published in 1836 in the literary journal *Sovremennik*.

This historical novel is dedicated to the events of the Pugachev's Rebellion in Russia in 1773-1775. It tells the story of a 17-years-old officer, Peter Grineff, sent by his father into military service. Peter was assigned to a small fortress of Belogorsk, where he fell in love with Maria, the daughter of the commandant...

This edition includes illustrations by Pavel Sokolov and other artists of 18-19th century: Borovikovski, Vladimirov, Ivanov and Perov.

Translation by T. Keane, 1894

Published by The Planet, 2011
© The Planet, 2011: book and cover design
www.the-planet-books.com

# Contents

Chapter I. The Sergeant of the Guards 4

Chapter II. The Guide 18

Chapter III. The Fortress 31

Chapter IV. The Duel 40

Chapter V. Love 51

Chapter VI. Pougatcheff 61

Chapter VII. The Assault 74

Chapter VIII. An Uninvited Guest 84

Chapter IX. The Parting 95

Chapter X. The Siege 101

Chapter XI. The Rebel Encampment 110

Chapter XII. The Orphan 123

Chapter XIII. The Arrest 132

Chapter XIV. The Sentence 141

# Chapter I.
# The Sergeant of the Guards

My father, Andrei Petrovitch Grineff, after having served in his youth under Count Münich,[1] quitted the service, in the year 17—, with the rank of senior major. He settled down upon his estate in the district of Simbirsk, where he married Avdotia Vassilevna U——, the daughter of a poor nobleman of the neighbourhood. Nine children were the result of this marriage. All my brothers and sisters died in their infancy. I was enrolled as a sergeant in the Semenovsky Regiment, through the influence of Prince B——, a major in the Guards and a near relation of our family. I was considered as being on leave of absence until the completion of my course of studies. In those days our system of education was very different from that in vogue at the present time. At five years of age I was given into the hands of our gamekeeper, Savelitch, whose sober conduct had rendered him worthy of being selected to take charge of me. Under his instruction, at the age of twelve, I could read and write Russian, and I was by no means a bad judge of the qualities of a greyhound. About that time my father engaged a Frenchman, a Monsieur Beaupré, who had been imported from Moscow, together with the yearly stock of wine and Provence oil. Savelitch

---

[1] A celebrated German general who entered the service of Russia during the reign of Peter the Great.

was not by any means pleased at his arrival.

"Heaven be thanked!" he muttered to himself; "the child is washed, combed, and well-fed. What need is there for spending money and engaging a Mossoo, as if there were not enough of our own people!"

Beaupré had been a hairdresser in his own country, then a soldier in Prussia; then he had come to Russia *pour être outchitel*,[1] without very well understanding the meaning of the word. He was a good sort of fellow, but extremely flighty and thoughtless. His chief weakness was a passion for the fair sex; but his tenderness not unfrequently met with rebuffs, which would cause him to sigh and lament for the whole twenty four hours. Moreover, to use his own expression, he was no enemy of the bottle, or, in other words, he loved to drink more than was good for him. But as, with us, wine was only served out at dinner, and then in small glasses only, and as, moreover, the teacher was generally passed over on these occasions, my Beaupré very soon became accustomed to Russian drinks, and even began to prefer them to the wines of his own country, as being more beneficial for the stomach. We soon became very good friends, and although, by the terms of the contract, he was engaged to teach me French, German, and all the sciences, yet he much preferred learning from me to chatter in Russian, and then each of us occupied himself with what seemed best to him. Our friendship was of the most intimate character, and I wished for no other mentor. But fate soon separated us, owing to an event which I will now proceed to relate.

The laundress, Palashka, a thick-set woman with a face scarred by the small-pox, and the one-eyed cowkeeper, Akoulka, made up their minds together one day and went and threw themselves at my mother's feet, accusing themselves of certain guilty weaknesses, complaining, with a flood of tears, that the Mossoo had taken advantage of their inexperience, and had effected their ruin. My mother did not look

---

[1] *Outchitel*. A tutor.

upon such matters in the light of a joke, so she consulted my father upon the subject. An inquiry into the matter was promptly resolved upon. He immediately sent for the rascally Frenchman. He was informed that Monsieur was engaged in giving me my lesson. My father came to my room. At that particular moment Beaupré was lying on the bed, sleeping the sleep of innocence. I was occupied in a very different manner. I ought to mention that a map had been obtained from Moscow, in order that I might be instructed in geography. It hung upon the wall without ever being made use of, and as it was a very large map, and the paper thick and of good quality, I had long been tempted to appropriate it to my own use. I resolved to make it into a kite, and, taking advantage of Beaupré's slumber, I set to work. My father entered the room just at the moment when I was adjusting a tail to the Cape of Good Hope.

*Artist P.P. Sokolov, 19th century*

Seeing me so occupied with geography, my father saluted me with a box on the ear, then stepped towards Beaupré, and waking him very unceremoniously, overwhelmed him with reproaches. In his confusion, Beaupré wanted to rise up from the bed, but he was unable to do so: the unfortunate

Frenchman was hopelessly intoxicated.

There was only one course to take after so many acts of misdemeanour. My father seized hold of him by the collar, lifted him off the bed, hustled him out of the room, and dismissed him that very same day from his service—to the unspeakable delight of Savelitch. Thus ended my education.

I now lived the life of a spoiled child, frightening the pigeons, and playing at leap-frog with the boys on the estate. I continued to lead this kind of life until I was sixteen years of age. Then came the turning-point in my existence.

One day in autumn, my mother was boiling some honey preserves in the parlour, and I was looking on and licking my lips as the liquid simmered and frothed. My father was sitting near the window, reading the *Court Calendar*, which he received every year. This book always had a great effect upon him; he used to read it with especial interest, and the reading of it always stirred his bile in the most astonishing manner. My mother, who was perfectly well acquainted with his whims and peculiarities, always endeavoured to keep this unfortunate book out of the way as much as she possibly could, and, on this account, his eyes would not catch a glimpse of the volume for months together. But when he did happen to find it, he would sit with it in his hands for hours at a stretch... As I have said, my father was reading the *Court Calendar*, every now and then shrugging his shoulders and muttering to himself: "Lieutenant-General!... He used to be a sergeant in my company!... Knight of both Russian Orders!... How long is it since we—"

At last my father flung the *Calendar* down upon the sofa, and sank into a reverie—a proceeding that was always of evil augury.

Suddenly he turned to my mother: "Avdotia Vassilevna,[1] how old is Petrousha[2]?"

---

[1] Avdotia, daughter of Basil.

[2] Diminutive of Peter.

*Artist P.P. Sokolov, 19th century*

"He is getting on for seventeen," replied my mother. "Petrousha was born in the same year that aunt Nastasia Gerasimovna[1] lost her eye, and —"

"Very well," said my father, interrupting her; "it is time

---

[1] Anastasia, daughter of Gerasim.

that he entered the service. He has had quite enough of running about the servants' rooms and climbing up to the dovecots."

The thought of soon having to part with me produced such an effect upon my mother, that she let the spoon fall into the saucepan, and the tears streamed down her cheeks. As for myself, it would be difficult to describe the delight that I felt. The thought of the service was associated in my mind with thoughts of freedom and the pleasures of a life in St. Petersburg. I imagined myself an officer in the Guards, that being, in my opinion, the summit of human felicity.

My father loved neither to change his intentions, nor to delay putting them into execution. The day for my departure was fixed. On the evening before, my father informed me that he intended to write to my future chief, and asked for pens and paper.

"Do not forget, Andrei Petrovitch[1]," said my mother, "to send my salutations to Prince B— —, and say that I hope he will take our Petrousha under his protection."

"What nonsense!" exclaimed my father, frowning. "Why should I write to Prince B— —?"

"Why, you said just now that you wanted to write to Petrousha's chief."

"Well, and what then?"

"Why, Prince B— — is Petrousha's chief. You know Petrousha is enrolled in the Semenovsky Regiment."

"Enrolled! What care I whether he is enrolled or not? Petrousha is not going to St. Petersburg. What would he learn by serving in St. Petersburg? To squander money and indulge in habits of dissipation. No, let him enter a regiment of the Line; let him learn to carry knapsack and belt, to smell powder, to become a soldier, and not an idler in the Guards. Where is his passport? Bring it here."

My mother went to get my passport, which she preserved in a small box along with the shirt in which I was

---

[1] The Russians usually address each other by their Christian name and that of their father. Thus Andrei Petrovitch means simply Andrew, son of Peter.

christened, and delivered it to my father with a trembling hand. My father read it through very attentively, placed it in front of him upon the table, and commenced to write his letter.

I was tortured with curiosity. Where was I to be sent to, if I was not going to St. Petersburg? I kept my eyes steadfastly fixed upon the pen, which moved slowly over the paper. At last he finished the letter, enclosed it in a cover along with my passport, took off his spectacles, and, calling me to him, said:

"Here is a letter for Andrei Karlovitch R— —, my old comrade and friend. You are going to Orenburg to serve under his command."

All my brilliant hopes were thus brought to the ground! Instead of a life of gaiety in St. Petersburg, there awaited me a tedious existence in a dreary and distant country. The service, which I had thought of with such rapture but a moment before, now presented itself to my eyes in the light of a great misfortune. But there was no help for it, and arguing the matter would have been of no avail.

Early the next morning a travelling carriage drew up before the door; my portmanteau was placed in it, as well as a small chest containing a tea-service and a tied-up cloth full of rolls and pies—the last tokens of home indulgence. My parents gave me their blessing. My father said to me:

"Good-bye, Peter! Serve faithfully whom you have sworn to serve; obey your superior officers; do not run after their favours; be not too eager in volunteering for service, but never shirk a duty when you are selected for it; and remember the proverb: 'Take care of your coat while it is new, and of your honour while it is young.'"

My mother, with tears in her eyes, enjoined me to take care of my health, at the same time impressing upon Savelitch to look well after the child. A cloak made of hare-skin was then put over my shoulders, and over that another made of fox-skin.

I seated myself in the carriage with Savelitch, and start-

*Artist P.P. Sokolov, 19th century*

ed off on my journey, weeping bitterly.

That same night I arrived at Simbirsk, where I was compelled to remain for the space of twenty four hours, to enable Savelitch to purchase several necessary articles which he had been commissioned to procure. I stopped at an inn. In the morning Savelitch sallied out to the shops. Tired of looking out of the window into a dirty alley, I began to wander about the rooms of the inn. As I entered the billiard-room, my eyes caught sight of a tall gentleman of about thirty five years of age, with long black moustaches; he was dressed in a morning-gown, and had a cue in his hand and a pipe between his teeth. He was playing with the marker, who drank a glass of brandy when he scored, but crept on all-fours beneath the table when he failed. I stopped to look at the game. The longer it continued, the more frequent became the crawling on all-fours, until at last the marker crept beneath the table and remained there.

The gentleman uttered a few strong expressions over him, as a sort of funeral oration, and then invited me to play a game with him. I declined, on the score that I did not know how to play. This evidently seemed very strange to him, and he looked at me with an air of commiseration. However, we soon fell into conversation. I learned that his name was Ivan Ivanovitch Zourin; that he was a captain in a Hussar regiment; that he was then stopping in Simbirsk, waiting to receive some recruits, and that he was staying at the same inn as myself.

Zourin invited me to dine with him, in military fashion, upon whatever Heaven should be pleased to set before us. I accepted his invitation with pleasure. We sat down to table. Zourin drank a great deal, and pressed me to do the same, saying that it was necessary for me to get accustomed to the ways of the service. He related to me several military anecdotes, which convulsed me with laughter, and when we rose from the table we had become intimate friends. Then he offered to teach me how to play at billiards.

"It is an indispensable game for soldiers like us," said he. "When on the march, for instance, you arrive at some insignificant village, what can you do to occupy the time? You cannot always be thrashing the Jews. You involuntarily make your way to the inn to play at billiards, and to do that, you must know how to play."

I was completely convinced, and I commenced to learn the game with great assiduity. Zourin encouraged me with loud-voiced praise, being astonished at my rapid progress; and after a few lessons he proposed that we should play for money, for the smallest sums possible, not for the sake of gain, but merely for the sake of not playing for nothing, which, according to his opinion, was an exceedingly bad habit.

*Artist P.P. Sokolov, 19th century*

I agreed to his proposal, and Zourin ordered a supply of punch, which he persuaded me to partake of, saying that it was necessary to become accustomed to it in the service; for what would the service be without punch! I followed his advice. In the meantime we continued our game. The more frequently I had recourse to the punch, the more emboldened I became. The balls kept continually flying in the wrong direction; I grew angry, abused the marker—who counted the points, Heaven only knows how,—increased the stakes from time to time—in a word, I behaved like a boy just out of leading-strings. In the meanwhile the time had passed away without my having observed it. Zourin glanced at the clock, laid down his cue, and informed me that I had lost a hundred roubles.[1] I was considerably confounded by this piece of information. My money was in the hands of Savelitch. I began to make some excuses. Zourin interrupted me:

"Pray, do not be uneasy. I can wait, and now let us go to Arinoushka[2]."

What more shall I add? I finished the day as foolishly as I had commenced it. We took supper with Arinoushka. Zourin kept continually filling my glass, observing as he did so, that it was necessary to become accustomed to it in the service. When I rose from the table, I was scarcely able to stand on my legs; at midnight, Zourin conducted me back to the inn.

Savelitch came to the doorstep to meet us. He uttered a groan on perceiving the indubitable signs of my zeal for the service.

"What has happened to you?" he said, in a voice of lamentation. "Where have you been drinking so? Oh, Lord! never did such a misfortune happen before!"

"Hold your tongue, you old greybeard!" I replied in an unsteady voice; "you are certainly drunk. Go to sleep… and put me to bed."

---

[1] The rouble, at that time, was worth about three shillings and four-pence.
[2] Diminutive of Arina.

The next morning I awoke with a violent headache, and with a confused recollection of the events of the day before. My reflections were interrupted by Savelitch, who brought me a cup of tea.

"You are beginning your games early, Peter Andreitch,[1]" he said, shaking his head. "And whom do you take after?"

As far as I know, neither your father nor grandfather were ever drunkards. As for your mother, I will say nothing; she has never drunk anything except *kvas*[2] since the day she was born. And who is to blame for all this? Why, it is that cursed Mossoo, who was ever running to Antipevna with: *'Madame, je vous prie, vodka.'* You see what a pretty pass your *je vous prie* has brought you to! There's no denying that the son of a dog taught you some nice things! It was worth while to hire such a heathen for your tutor, as if our master had not enough of his own people!"

I felt ashamed of myself. I turned my back to him, and said:

"Go away, Savelitch; I do not want any tea."

But it was a difficult matter to quiet Savelitch when he had set his mind upon preaching a sermon.

"You see now, Peter Andreitch, what it is to get drunk. You have a headache, and you do not want to eat or drink anything. A man who gets drunk is good for nothing. Have some cucumber pickle with honey; or perhaps half a glass of fruit wine would be better still. What do you say?"

At that moment a boy entered the room and handed me a note from Zourin. I opened it and read the following lines:

"Dear Peter Andreivitch,

"Be so good as to send me, by my boy, the hundred roubles which you lost to me yesterday. I am in great need of money.

"Yours faithfully,
"Ivan Zourin."

---

[1] Peter, son of Andrew.

[2] A sour but refreshing drink made from rye-meal and malt.

There was no help for it. I assumed an air of indifference, and turning to Savelitch, who was my treasurer and caretaker in one, I ordered him to give the boy a hundred roubles.

"What? why?" asked the astonished Savelitch.

"I owe them to him," I replied, with the greatest possible coolness.

"Owe!" ejaculated Savelitch, becoming more and more astonished. "When did you get into his debt? It looks a very suspicious piece of business. You may do as you like, my lord, but I shall not give the money." I thought that, if in this decisive moment I did not gain the upper hand of the obstinate old man, it would be difficult for me to liberate myself from his tutelage later on; so, looking haughtily at him, I said:

"I am your master, and you are my servant. The money is mine. I played and lost it because I chose to do so; and I advise you not to oppose my wishes, but to do what you are ordered."

Savelitch was so astounded at my words, that he clasped his hands and stood as if petrified.

"What are you standing there like that for?" I exclaimed angrily.

Savelitch began to weep. "Father, Peter Andreitch," he stammered in a quivering voice, "do not break my heart with grief. You are the light of my life, so listen to me—to an old man: write to this robber, and tell him that you were only joking, that we have not got so much money. A hundred roubles! Merciful Heaven! Tell him that your parents have strictly forbidden you to play for anything except nuts—"

"That will do; let me have no more of your chatter! Give me the money, or I will put you out by the neck!"

Savelitch looked at me with deep sadness, and went for the money. I pitied the poor old man; but I wanted to assert my independence and to show that I was no longer a child.

The money was paid to Zourin. Savelitch hastened to get me away from the accursed inn. He made his appearance with the information that the horses were ready. With an uneasy conscience, and a silent feeling of remorse, I left Simbirsk without taking leave of my teacher of billiards, and without thinking that I should ever see him again.

# Chapter II.
# The Guide

My reflections during the journey were not very agreeable. My loss, according to the value of money at that time, was of no little importance. I could not but confess, within my own mind, that my behaviour at the Simbirsk inn was very stupid, and I felt guilty in the presence of Savelitch. All this tormented me. The old man sat in gloomy silence upon the seat of the vehicle, with his face averted from me, and every now and then giving vent to a sigh. I wanted at all hazards to become reconciled to him, but I did not know how to begin. At last I said to him:

"Come, come, Savelitch, that will do, let us be friends. I was to blame; I see myself that I was in the wrong. I acted very foolishly yesterday, and I offended you without cause. I promise that I will act more wisely for the future, and listen to your advice. Come, don't be angry, but let us be friends again."

"Ah! father, Peter Andreitch," he replied, with a deep sigh, "I am angry with myself; I alone am to blame. How could I leave you alone in the inn! But what else could be expected? We are led astray by sin. The thought came into my mind to go and see the clerk's wife, who is my gossip.[1] But so it was: I went to my gossip, and ill-luck came of it. Was there ever such a misfortune! How shall I ever be able to look in the face of my master and mistress? What will they say when they know that their child is a drunkard and

---

[1] Savelitch uses the word here in its old meaning of fellow-sponsor.

a gambler?"

In order to console poor Savelitch, I gave him my word that I would never again spend a single copeck[1] without his consent. He calmed down by degrees, although every now and again he still continued muttering, with a shake of the head, "A hundred roubles! It's no laughing matter!"

I was nearing the place of my destination. On every side of me extended a dreary-looking plain, intersected by hills and ravines. Everything was covered with snow. The sun was setting. The *kibitka*[2] was proceeding along the narrow road, or, to speak more precisely, along the track made by the peasants' sledges. Suddenly the driver began gazing intently about him, and at last, taking off his cap, he turned to me and said:

"My lord, will you not give orders to turn back?"

"Why?"

"The weather does not look very promising: the wind is beginning to rise; see how it whirls the freshly fallen snow along."

"What does that matter?"

"And do you see that yonder?"

And the driver pointed with his whip towards the east.

"I see nothing, except the white steppe and the clear sky."

"There—away in the distance: that cloud."

I perceived, indeed, on the edge of the horizon, a white cloud, which I had taken at first for a distant hill. The driver explained to me that this small cloud presaged a snowstorm.

I had heard of the snowstorms of that part of the country, and I knew that whole trains of waggons were frequently buried in the drifts. Savelitch was of the same opinion as the driver, and advised that we should return. But the wind did not seem to me to be very strong: I hoped to be able to reach the next station in good time, and I gave orders to drive on faster.

---

[1] Russian copper coin.

[2] A kind of rough travelling cart.

The driver urged on the horses at a gallop, but he still continued to gaze towards the east. The horses entered into their work with a will. In the meantime the wind had gradually increased in violence. The little cloud had changed into a large, white, nebulous mass, which rose heavily, and gradually began to extend over the whole sky. A fine snow began to fall, and then all at once this gave place to large heavy flakes. The wind roared; the snowstorm had burst upon us. In one moment the dark sky became confounded with the sea of snow; everything had disappeared.

"Well, my lord," cried the driver, "this is a misfortune; it is a regular snowstorm!"

I looked out of the *kibitka*; all was storm and darkness. The wind blew with such terrific violence that it seemed as if it were endowed with life. Savelitch and I were covered with snow: the horses ploughed their way onward at a walking pace, and soon came to a standstill.

"Why don't you go on?" I called out impatiently to the driver.

"But where am I to drive to?" he replied, jumping down from his seat; "I haven't the slightest idea as to where we are; there is no road, and it is dark all round."

I began to scold him. Savelitch took his part.

"You ought to have taken his advice," he said angrily. "You should have returned to the posting-house; you could have had some tea and could have slept there till the morning; the storm would have blown over by that time, and then you could have proceeded on your journey. And why such haste? It would be all very well if we were going to a wedding!"

Savelitch was right. But what was to be done? The snow still continued to fall. A drift began to form around the *kibitka*. The horses stood with dejected heads, and every now and then a shudder shook their frames. The driver kept walking round them, and, being unable to do anything else, busied himself with adjusting the harness. Savelitch grumbled. I looked round on every side, hoping to discover some sign of a house or a road, but I could distinguish nothing except the confused whirling snowdrifts... Suddenly I caught sight of something black.

"Hillo! driver," I cried; "look! what is that black object yonder?"

The driver looked carefully in the direction indicated.

"God knows, my lord," said he, seating himself in his place again; "it is neither a sledge nor a tree, and it seems to move. It must be either a man or a wolf."

I ordered him to drive towards the unknown object, which was gradually drawing nearer to us. In about two minutes we came up to it and discovered it to be a man.

"Hi! my good man," cried the driver to him; "say, do you know where the road is?"

"The road is here; I am standing on a firm track," replied the wayfarer. "But what of it?"

"Listen, peasant," said I to him; "do you know this country? Can you lead me to a place where I can obtain a night's lodging?"

"I know the country very well," replied the peasant. "Heaven be thanked, I have crossed it and re-crossed it in every direction. But you see what sort of weather it is: it would be very easy to miss the road. You had much better stay here and wait; perhaps the storm will blow over, and the sky become clear, then we shall be able to find the road by the help of the stars."

His cool indifference encouraged me. I had already resolved to abandon myself to the will of God and to pass the night upon the steppe, when suddenly the peasant mounted to the seat of our vehicle and said to the driver:

"Thank Heaven, there is a house not far off; turn to the right and go straight on."

"Why should I go to the right?" asked the driver in a dissatisfied tone. "Where do you see a road? I am not the owner of these horses that I should use the whip without mercy."

The driver seemed to me to be in the right.

"In truth," said I, "why do you think that there is a

house not far off?"

"Because the wind blows from that direction," replied the wayfarer, "and I can smell smoke; that is a sign that there is a village close at hand."

His sagacity and nicety of smell astonished me. I ordered the driver to go on. The horses moved heavily through the deep snow. The *kibitka* advanced very slowly, at one moment mounting to the summit of a ridge, at another sinking into a deep hollow, now rolling to one side, and now to the other. It was very much like being in a ship on a stormy sea. Savelitch sighed and groaned, and continually jostled against me. I let down the cover of the *kibitka*, wrapped myself up in my cloak, and fell into a slumber, lulled by the music of the storm, and rocked by the motion of the vehicle.

I had a dream which I shall never forget, and in which I still see something prophetic when I compare it with the strange events of my life. The reader will excuse me for mentioning the matter, for probably he knows from experience that man is naturally given to superstition in spite of the great contempt entertained for it.

I was in that condition of mind when reality and imagination become confused in the vague sensations attending the first stage of drowsiness. It seemed to me that the storm still continued, and that we were still wandering about the wilderness of snow... All at once I caught sight of a gate, and we entered the courtyard of our mansion. My first thought was a fear that my father would be angry with me for my involuntary return to the paternal roof, and would regard it as an act of intentional disobedience. With a feeling of uneasiness I sprang out of the *kibitka*, and saw my mother coming down the steps to meet me, with a look of deep affliction upon her face.

"Hush!" she said to me; "your father is on the point of death, and wishes to take leave of you."

Struck with awe, I followed her into the bedroom. I looked about me; the room was dimly lighted, and round the bed stood several persons with sorrow-stricken countenances. I approached very gently; my mother raised the curtain and said:

"Andrei Petrovitch, Petrousha has arrived; he has returned because he heard of your illness; give him your blessing."

I knelt down and fixed my eyes upon the face of the sick man. But what did I see?... Instead of my father, I saw lying in the bed a black-bearded peasant, who looked at me with an expression of gaiety upon his countenance. Greatly perplexed, I turned round to my mother and said to her:

"What does all this mean? This is not my father. Why should I ask this peasant for his blessing?"

"It is all the same, Petrousha," replied my mother; "he is your stepfather; kiss his hand and let him bless you."

I would not consent to it. Then the peasant sprang out of bed, grasped the axe which hung at his back,[1] and commenced nourishing it about on every side. I wanted to run away, but I could not; the room began to get filled with dead bodies; I kept stumbling against them, and my feet continually slipped in pools of blood. The dreadful peasant called out to me in a gentle voice, saying:

"Do not be afraid; come and receive my blessing."

Terror and doubt took possession of me... At that moment I awoke; the horses had come to a standstill. Savelitch took hold of my hand, saying:

"Get out, my lord, we have arrived."

"Where are we?" I asked, rubbing my eyes.

"At a place of refuge. God came to our help and conducted us straight to the fence of the house. Get out as quickly as you can, my lord, and warm yourself."

I stepped out of the *kibitka*. The storm still raged, although with less violence than at first. It was as dark as if we were totally blind. The host met us at the door, holding a lantern under the skirt of his coat, and conducted me into a room, small, but tolerably clean. It was lit up by a pine torch.

---

[1] The Russian peasant usually carries his axe behind him.

On the wall hung a long rifle, and a tall Cossack cap.

The host, a Yaikian Cossack by birth, was a peasant of about sixty years of age, still hale and strong. Savelitch brought in the tea-chest, and asked for a fire in order to prepare some tea, which I seemed to need at that moment more than at any other time in my life. The host hastened to attend to the matter.

"Where is the guide?" I said to Savelitch.

"Here, your Excellency," replied a voice from above.

I glanced up at the loft, and saw a black beard and two sparkling eyes.

*Artist P.P. Sokolov, 19th century*

"Well, friend, are you cold?"

"How could I be otherwise than cold in only a thin tunic! I had a fur coat, but why should I hide my fault?—I pawned it yesterday with a brandy-seller; the cold did not seem to be so severe."

At that moment the host entered with a smoking tea-urn; I offered our guide a cup of tea; the peasant came down from the loft. His exterior seemed to me somewhat remarkable. He was about forty years of age, of middle height, thin and broad-shouldered. In his black beard streaks of grey were beginning to make their appearance; his large, lively black eyes were incessantly on the roll. His face had something rather agreeable about it, although an expression of vindictiveness could also be detected upon it. His hair was cut close round his head. He was dressed in a ragged tunic and Tartar trousers. I gave him a cup of tea; he tasted it, and made a wry face.

"Your Excellency," said he, "be so good as to order a glass of wine for me; tea is not the drink for us Cossacks."

I willingly complied with his request. The landlord brought a square bottle and a glass from a cupboard, went up to him, and, looking into his face, said:

"Oh! you are again in our neighbourhood! Where have you come from?"

My guide winked significantly, and made reply:

"Flying in the garden, pecking hempseed; the old woman threw a stone, but it missed its aim. And how is it with you?"

"How is it with us?" replied the landlord, continuing the allegorical conversation, "they were beginning to ring the vespers, but the pope's wife would not allow it: the pope is on a visit, and the devils are in the glebe."

"Hold your tongue, uncle," replied my rover; "when there is rain, there will be mushrooms; and when there are mushrooms, there will be a pannier; but now" (and here he winked again) "put your axe behind your back; the ranger is going about. Your Excellency, I drink to your health!"

With these words he took hold of the glass, made the sign of the cross, and drank off the liquor in one draught; then, bowing to me, he returned to the loft.

At that time I could not understand anything of this thieves' slang, but afterwards I understood that it referred to the Yaikian army, which had only just then been reduced to submission after the revolt of 1772. Savelitch listened with a look of great dissatisfaction. He glanced very suspiciously, first at the landlord, then at the guide. The inn, or *umet*, as it was called in those parts, was situated in the middle of the steppe, far from every habitation or village, and had very much the appearance of a rendezvous for thieves. But there was no help for it. We could not think of continuing our journey. The uneasiness of Savelitch afforded me very great amusement. In the meantime I made all necessary arrangements for passing the night comfortably, and then stretched myself upon a bench. Savelitch resolved to avail himself of the stove[1]; our host lay down upon the floor. Soon all in the house were snoring, and I fell into a sleep as sound as that of the grave.

When I awoke on the following morning, at a somewhat late hour, I perceived that the storm was over. The sun was shining. The snow lay like a dazzling shroud over the boundless steppe. The horses were harnessed. I paid the reckoning to the host, the sum asked of us being so very moderate that even Savelitch did not dispute the matter and commence to haggle about the payment as was his usual custom; moreover, his suspicions of the previous evening had completely vanished from his mind. I called for our guide, thanked him for the assistance he had rendered us, and ordered Savelitch to give him half a rouble for brandy.

Savelitch frowned.

"Half a rouble for brandy?" said he; "why so? Because you were pleased to bring him with you to this inn? With your leave, my lord, but we have not too many half roubles to spare. If we give money for brandy to everybody we have to deal with, we shall very soon have to starve ourselves."

I could not argue with Savelitch. According to my own promise, the disposal of my money was to be left entirely to his discretion. But I felt rather vexed that I was not able to show my gratitude to a man who, if he had not rescued me from certain destruction, had at least delivered me from a very disagreeable position.

---

[1] The usual sleeping place of the Russian peasant.

"Well," said I, coldly, "if you will not give him half a rouble, give him something out of my wardrobe; he is too thinly clad. Give him my hare-skin pelisse."

"In the name of Heaven, father, Peter Andreitch!" said Savelitch, "why give him your pelisse? The dog will sell it for drink at the first tavern that he comes to."

"It is no business of yours, old man," said my stroller, "whether I sell it for drink or not. His Excellency is pleased to give me a cloak from off his own shoulders; it is his lordly will, and it is your duty, as servant, to obey, and not to dispute."

"Have you no fear of God, you robber!" said Savelitch, in an angry tone. "You see that the child has not yet reached the age of discretion, and yet you are only too glad to take advantage of his good-nature, and rob him. What do you want with my master's pelisse? You will not be able to stretch it across your accursed shoulders."

"I beg of you not to show off your wit," I said to my

*Artist P.P. Sokolov, 19th century*

27

guardian. "Bring the pelisse hither immediately!"

"Gracious Lord!" groaned Savelitch, "the pelisse is almost brand-new! If it were to anybody deserving of it, it would be different, but to give it to a ragged drunkard!"

However, the pelisse was brought. The peasant instantly commenced to try it on. And, indeed, the garment, which I had grown out of, and which was rather tight for me, was a great deal too small for him. But he contrived to get it on somehow, though not without bursting the seams in the effort. Savelitch very nearly gave vent to a groan when he heard the stitches giving way.

The stroller was exceedingly pleased with my present. He conducted me to the *kibitka* and said, with a low bow:

"Many thanks, your Excellency! May God reward you for your virtue. I shall never forget your kindness."

He went his way, and I set out again on my journey, without paying any attention to Savelitch, and I soon forgot all about the storm of the previous day, the guide, and my pelisse.

On arriving at Orenburg, I immediately presented myself to the general. He was a tall man, but somewhat bent with age. His long hair was perfectly white. His old faded uniform recalled to mind the warrior of the time of the Empress Anne, and he spoke with a strong German accent.

I gave him the letter from my father. On hearing the name, he glanced at me quickly.

"Mein Gott!" said he, "it does not seem so very long ago since Andrei Petrovitch was your age, and now what a fine young fellow he has got for a son! Ach! time, time!"

He opened the letter and began to read it half aloud, making his own observations upon it in the course of his reading.

"'Esteemed Sir, Ivan Karlovitch, I hope that your Excellency'—Why all this ceremony? Pshaw! Isn't he ashamed of himself? To be sure, discipline before everything, but is that the way to write to an old comrade?—'Your Excellency has not forgotten'—Hm!—'and—when—with the late

Field Marshal Mün—in the campaign—also Caroline'—Ha, brother! he still remembers our old pranks, then?—'Now to business.—I send you my young hopeful'—Hm!—'Hold him with hedgehog mittens.'—What are hedgehog mittens? That must be a Russian proverb.—What does 'hold him with hedgehog mittens' mean?" he repeated, turning to me.

*Artist P.P. Sokolov, 19th century*

"It means," I replied, looking as innocent as I possibly could, "to treat a person kindly, not to be too severe, and to allow as much liberty as possible."

"Hm! I understand—'And do not give him too much liberty.'—No, it is evident that 'hedgehog mittens' does not mean that.—'Enclosed you will find his passport.'—Where is it then? Ah! here it is.—'Enrol him in the Semenovsky Regiment'—Very well, very well, everything shall be attended to.—'Allow me without ceremony to embrace you as an old comrade and friend.'—Ah! at last he has got to it.—'Etcetera, etcetera.'—Well, my little father[1]," said he, finishing the reading of the letter, and putting my passport on one side, "everything shall be arranged; you shall be an officer in the — — Regiment, and so that you may lose no time, start tomorrow for the fortress of Belogorsk, where you will be under the command of Captain Mironoff, a good and honest man. There you will learn real service, and be taught what real discipline is. Orenburg is not the place for you, there is nothing for you to do there; amusements are injurious to a young man. Favour me with your company at dinner today."

"This is getting worse and worse," I thought to myself. "Of what use will it be to me to have been a sergeant in the Guards almost from my mother's womb! Whither has it led me? To the — — Regiment, and to a dreary fortress on the borders of the Kirghis-Kaisaks steppes!"

I dined with Andrei Karlovitch, in company with his old adjutant. A strict German economy ruled his table, and I believe that the fear of being obliged to entertain an additional guest now and again was partly the cause of my being so promptly banished to the garrison.

The next day I took leave of the general, and set out for the place of my destination.

---

[1] Little father *(batyushka)*. A familiar idiom peculiar to the Russian language.

# Chapter III.
# The Fortress

The fortress of Belogorsk was situated about forty versts[1] from Orenburg. The road to it led along the steep bank of the Yaik.[2] The river was not yet frozen, and its leaden-coloured waves had a dark and melancholy aspect as they rose and fell between the dreary banks covered with the white snow. Beyond it stretched the Kirghis steppes. I sank into reflections, most of them of a gloomy nature. Garrison life had little attraction for me. I endeavoured to picture to myself Captain Mironoff, my future chief; and I imagined him to be a severe, ill-tempered old man, knowing nothing except what was connected with his duty, and ready to arrest me and put me on bread and water for the merest trifle.

In the meantime it began to grow dark, and we quickened our pace.

"Is it far to the fortress?" I inquired of our driver.

"Not far," he replied, "you can see it yonder."

I looked around on every side, expecting to see formidable bastions, towers, and ramparts, but I could see nothing except a small village surrounded by a wooden palisade. On one side stood three or four hayricks, half covered with snow; on the other a crooked looking windmill, with its bark sails hanging idly down.

"But where is the fortress?" I asked in astonishment.

"There it is," replied the driver, pointing to the village,

---

[1] A verst is two-thirds of an English mile.

[2] A tributary of the Ural.

and, as he spoke, we entered into it.

At the gate I saw an old cast-iron gun; the streets were narrow and crooked; the cottages small, and for the most part covered with thatch. I expressed a wish to be taken to the Commandant, and, in about a minute, the *kibitka* stopped in front of a small wooden house, built on an eminence, and situated near the church, which was likewise of wood.

Nobody came out to meet me. I made my way to the entrance and then proceeded to the ante-room. An old pensioner, seated at a table, was engaged in sewing a blue patch on the elbow of a green uniform coat. I ordered him to announce me.

"Go inside, little father," replied the pensioner; "our people are at home."

I entered into a very clean room, furnished in the old-fashioned style. In one corner stood a cupboard containing earthenware utensils; on the wall hung an officer's diploma, framed and glazed, and around it were arranged a few rude wood engravings, representing the "Capture of Kustrin and Otchakoff,"[1] the "Choice of the Bride," and the "Burial of the Cat." At the window sat an old woman in a jerkin, and wearing a handkerchief round her head. She was unwinding thread which a one-eyed old man, dressed in an officer's uniform, held in his outstretched hands.

"What is your pleasure, little father?" she asked, continuing her occupation.

I replied that I had come to enter the service, and, in accordance with the regulations, to notify my arrival to the Captain in command. And with these words I turned towards the one-eyed old man, whom I supposed to be the Commandant; but the old lady interrupted me in the speech which I had so carefully prepared beforehand.

"Ivan Kouzmitch[2] is not at home," said she; "he has gone to visit Father Gerasim. But it is all the same, I am his wife."

---

[1] Taken from the Turks in 1737 by the Russian troops under Count Münich.

[2] Ivan, son of Kouzma.

*Artist P.P. Sokolov, 19th century*

She summoned a maid-servant and told her to call an orderly officer. The little old man looked at me out of his one eye with much curiosity.

"May I ask," said he, "in what regiment you have deigned to serve?"

I satisfied his curiosity.

"And may I ask," he continued, "why you have exchanged the Guards for this garrison?"

I replied that such was the wish of the authorities.

"Probably for conduct unbecoming an officer of the Guards?" continued the indefatigable interrogator.

"A truce to your foolish chatter," said the Captain's wife to him; "you see that the young man is tired after his journey. He has something else to do than to listen to your nonsense." Then turning to me she added: "You are not the first, and you will not be the last. It is a hard life here, but you will soon get to like it. It is five years ago since Shvabrin Alexei Ivanitch was sent here to us for a murder. Heaven knows what it was that caused him to go wrong. You see, he went out of the town with a lieutenant; they had taken their swords with them, and they began to thrust at one another, and Alexei Ivanitch stabbed the lieutenant, and all before two witnesses! But what would you? Man is not master of sin."

At this moment the orderly officer, a young and well-built Cossack, entered the room.

"Maximitch," said the Captain's wife to him, "conduct this officer to his quarters, and see that everything is attended to."

"I obey, Vassilissa Egorovna," replied the orderly. "Is not his Excellency to lodge with Ivan Polejaeff?"

"What a booby you are, Maximitch!" said the Captain's wife. "Polejaeff's house is crowded already; besides, he is my gossip, and remembers that we are his superiors. Take the officer—what is your name, little father?"

"Peter Andreitch."

"Take Peter Andreitch to Simon Kouzoff. The rascal allowed his horse to get in my kitchen-garden... And is everything right, Maximitch?"

"Everything, thank God!" replied the Cossack; "only Corporal Prokhoroff has been having a squabble at the bath with Ustinia Pegoulina, on account of a can of hot water."

"Ivan Ignatitch," said the Captain's wife to the one-eyed old man, "decide between Prokhoroff and Ustinia as to who is right and who is wrong, and then punish both. Now, Maximitch, go, and God be with you. Peter Andreitch, Maximitch will conduct you to your quarters."

I bowed and took my departure. The orderly conducted me to a hut, situated on the steep bank of the river, at the extreme end of the fortress. One half of the hut was occupied by the family of Simon Kouzoff; the other was given up to me. It consisted of one room, of tolerable cleanliness, and was divided into two by a partition.

Savelitch began to set the room in order, and I looked out of the narrow window. Before me stretched a gloomy steppe. On one side stood a few huts, and two or three fowls were wandering about the street. An old woman, standing on a doorstep with a trough in her hands, was calling some pigs, which answered her with friendly grunts. And this was the place in which I was condemned to spend my youth! Grief took possession of me; I came away from the window and lay down to sleep without eating any supper, in spite of the exhortations of Savelitch, who kept repeating in a tone of distress:

"Lord of heaven! he will eat nothing! What will my mistress say if the child falls ill?"

The next morning I had scarcely begun to dress when the door opened, and a young officer, somewhat short in stature, with a swarthy and rather ill-looking countenance, though distinguished by extraordinary vivacity, entered the room.

"Pardon me," he said to me in French, "for coming without ceremony to make your acquaintance. I heard yesterday of your arrival, and the desire to see at last a fresh human face took such possession of me, that I could not wait any longer. You will understand this when you have lived here a little while."

I conjectured that this was the officer who had been dismissed from the Guards on account of the duel. We soon became acquainted. Shvabrin was by no means a fool. His conversation was witty and entertaining. With great liveliness he described to me the family of the Commandant, his society, and the place to which fate had conducted me. I was laughing with all my heart when the old soldier who had been mending his uniform in the Commandant's antechamber, came to me, and, in the name of Vassilissa Egorovna, invited me to dinner. Shvabrin declared that he would go with me.

On approaching the Commandant's house, we perceived on the square about twenty old soldiers, with long pig-tails and three-cornered hats. They were standing to the front. Before them stood the Commandant, a tall and sprightly old man, in a nightcap and flannel dressing-gown. Observing us, he came forward towards us, said a few kind words to me, and then went on again with the drilling of his men. We were going to stop to watch the evolutions, but he requested us to go to Vassilissa Egorovna, promising to join us in a little while. "Here," he added, "there is nothing for you to see."

*Artist P.P. Sokolov, 19th century*

Vassilissa Egorovna received us with unfeigned glad-ness and simplicity, and treated me as if she had known me all my life. The pensioner and Palashka spread the table-cloth.

"What is detaining my Ivan Kouzmitch so long today?" said the Commandant's wife. "Palashka, go and call your master to dinner... But where is Masha[1]?"

At that moment there entered the room a young girl of about eighteen years of age, with a round, rosy face, and light brown hair, brushed smoothly back behind her ears,

---

[1] Diminutive of Maria or Mary.

which were tinged with a deep blush. She did not produce a very favourable impression upon me at the first glance. I regarded her with prejudiced eyes. Shvabrin had described Masha, the Captain's daughter, as a perfect idiot. Maria Ivanovna[1] sat down in a corner and began to sew. Meanwhile, the cabbage-soup was brought in. Vassilissa Egorovna, not seeing her husband, sent Palashka after him a second time.

"Tell your master that the guests are waiting, and that the soup is getting cold. Thank Heaven, the drill will not run away! he will have plenty of time to shout himself hoarse."

The Captain soon made his appearance, accompanied by the little one-eyed old man.

"What is the meaning of this, little father?" said his wife to him; "the dinner has been ready a long time, and you would not come."

"Why, you see, Vassilissa Egorovna," said Ivan Kouzmitch, "I was occupied with my duties; I was teaching my little soldiers."

"Nonsense!" replied his wife; "it is all talk about your teaching the soldiers. The service does not suit them, and you yourself don't understand anything about it. It would be better for you to stay at home and pray to God. My dear guests, pray take your places at the table."

We sat down to dine. Vassilissa Egorovna was not silent for a single moment, and she overwhelmed me with questions. Who were my parents? Were they living? Where did they live? How much were they worth? On hearing that my father owned three hundred souls[2]:

"Really now!" she exclaimed; "well, there are some rich people in the world! As for us, my little father, we have only our one servant-girl, Palashka; but, thank God, we manage to get along well enough! There is only one thing that we are troubled about. Masha is an eligible girl, but what has she

---

[1] Mary, daughter of Ivan (i.e., Masha).

[2] The technical name for serfs.

got for a marriage portion? A clean comb, a hand-broom, and three copecks—Heaven have pity upon her!—to pay for a bath. If she can find a good man, all very well; if not, she will have to be an old maid."

I glanced at Maria Ivanovna; she was blushing all over, and tears were even falling into her plate. I began to feel pity for her, and I hastened to change the conversation.

"I have heard," said I, as appropriately as I could, "that the Bashkirs are assembling to make an attack upon your fortress."

"And from whom did you hear that, my little father?" asked Ivan Kouzmitch. I "They told me so in Orenburg," I replied.

"All nonsense!" said the Commandant; "we have heard nothing about them for a long time. The Bashkirs are a timid lot, and the Kirghises have learnt a lesson. Don't be alarmed, they will not attack us; but if they should venture to do so, we will teach them such a lesson that they will not make another move for the next ten years."

"And are you not afraid," continued I, turning to the Captain's wife, "to remain in a fortress exposed to so many dangers?"

"Habit, my little father," she replied. "It is twenty years ago since they transferred us from the regiment to this place, and you cannot imagine how these accursed heathens used to terrify me. If I caught a glimpse of their hairy caps now and then, or if I heard their yells, will you believe it, my father, my heart would leap almost into my mouth. But now I am so accustomed to it that I would toot move out of my place if anyone came to tell me that the villains were prowling round the fortress."

"Vassilissa Egorovna is a very courageous lady," observed Shvabrin earnestly; "Ivan Kouzmitch can bear witness to that."

"Yes, I believe you," said Ivan Kouzmitch; "the wife is not one of the timid ones."

"And Maria Ivanovna," I asked, "is she as brave as you?"

"Masha brave?" replied her mother. "No, Masha is a coward. Up to the present time she has never been able to hear the report of a gun without trembling all over. Two years ago, when Ivan Kouzmitch took the idea into his head to fire off our cannon on my name-day[1], my little dove was so frightened that she nearly died through terror. Since then we have never fired off the accursed cannon."

We rose from the table. The Captain and his wife went to indulge in a nap, and I accompanied Shvabrin to his quarters, where I spent the whole evening.

---

[1] The day kept in honour of the saint after whom one is called.

# Chapter IV.
# The Duel

Several weeks passed by, and my life in the fortress of Belogorsk became not only endurable, but even agreeable. In the house of the Commandant I was received as one of the family. Both husband and wife were very worthy persons. Ivan Kouzmitch, who had risen from the ranks, was a simple and unaffected man, but exceedingly honest and good-natured. His wife managed things generally for him, and this was quite in harmony with his easygoing disposition. Vassilissa Egorovna looked after the business of the service as well as her own domestic affairs, and ruled the fortress precisely as she did her own house. Maria Ivanovna soon ceased to be shy in my presence. We became acquainted. I found her a sensible and feeling girl. In an imperceptible manner I became attached to this good family, even to Ivan Ignatitch, the one-eyed garrison lieutenant, whom Shvabrin accused of being on terms of undue intimacy with Vassilissa Egorovna, an accusation which had not a shadow of probability to give countenance to it; but Shvabrin did not trouble himself about that.

I was promoted to the rank of officer. My duties were not very heavy. In this God-protected fortress there was neither parade, nor drill, nor guard-mounting. The Commandant sometimes instructed the soldiers for his own amusement, but he had not yet got so far as teaching them which was the right-hand side and which the left. Shvabrin had several French books in his possession. I began to read them, and this awakened within me a taste for literature. In the morning I read, exercised myself in translating, and sometimes even attempted to compose verses. I dined nearly always at the Commandant's, where I generally spent the rest of the day, and where sometimes of an evening came Father Gerasim, with his wife, Akoulina Pamphilovna, the greatest gossip in the whole neighbourhood. It is unnecessary for me to mention that Shvabrin and I saw each other every day, but his conversation began to be more disagreeable the more I saw of him. His continual ridiculing of the Commandant's family, and especially his sarcastic observations concerning Maria Ivanovna, annoyed me exceedingly. There was no other society in the fortress, and I wished for no other.

In spite of the predictions, the Bashkirs did not revolt. Tranquillity reigned around our fortress. But the peace was suddenly disturbed by civil dissensions.

I have already mentioned that I occupied myself with literature. My essays were tolerable for those days, and Alexander Petrovitch Soumarokoff,[1] some years afterwards, praised them very much. One day I contrived to write a little song with which I was much pleased. It is well-known that, under the appearance of asking advice, authors frequently endeavour to secure a well-disposed listener. And so, writing out my little song, I took it to Shvabrin, who was the only person in the whole fortress who could appreciate a poetical production. After a short preamble, I drew my manuscript out of my pocket, and read to him the following verses:

> "I banish thoughts of love, and try
> My fair one to forget;
> And, to be free again,
> I fly from Masha with regret.

---

[1] A Russian dramatic poet, once celebrated, but then almost forgotten. His most popular works were two tragedies, "Khoreff," and "Demetrius the Pretender."

"My troubled soul no rest can know,
No peace of mind for me;
For wheresoever I may go,
Those eyes I still shall see.

"Take pity, Masha, on this heart
Oppressed by grief and care;
And let compassion rend apart
The clouds of dark despair."

"What do you think of it?" I asked Shvabrin, expecting that praise which I considered I was justly entitled to. But, to ray great disappointment, Shvabrin, who was generally complaisant", declared very peremptorily that the verses were not worth much.

"And why?" I asked, hiding my vexation.

"Because," he replied, "such verses are worthy of my instructor Tredyakovsky,[1] and remind me very much of his love couplets."

Then he took the manuscript from me and began unmercifully to pull to pieces every verse and word, jeering at me in the most sarcastic manner. This was more than I could endure, and snatching my manuscript out of his hand, I told him that I would never show him any more of my compositions. Shvabrin laughed at my threat.

"We shall see," said he, "if you will keep your word. A poet needs a listener, just as Ivan Kouzmitch needs his decanter of brandy before dinner. And who is this Masha to whom you declare your tender passion and your amorous distress? Can it be Maria Ivanovna?"

"That is not your business," replied I, frowning; "it is nothing to do with you who she is. I want neither your opinion nor your conjectures."

"Oho! my vain poet and discreet lover!" continued Shvabrin, irritating me more and more. "But listen to a friend's advice; if you wish to succeed, I advise you not to have re-

---

[1] A Russian poet of the 18th century.

course to writing verses."

"What do you mean, sir? Please explain yourself."

"With pleasure. I mean that if you wish Masha Mironoff to meet you at dusk, instead of tender verses, you must make her a present of a pair of earrings."

My blood began to boil.

"Why have you such an opinion of her?" I asked, with difficulty restraining my anger.

"Because," replied he, with a fiendish smile, "I know from experience her ways and habits."

"You lie, scoundrel!" I exclaimed with fury. "You lie in the most shameless manner!"

Shvabrin changed colour.

"This shall not be overlooked," said he, pressing my hand. "You shall give me satisfaction."

"With pleasure, whenever you like," I replied, delighted beyond measure.

At that moment I was ready to tear him in pieces.

I immediately hastened to Ivan Ignatitch, and found him with a needle in his hand; in obedience to the commands of the Commandant's wife he was stringing mushrooms for drying during the winter.

"Ah, Peter Andreitch," said he, on seeing me, "you are welcome. May I ask on what business Heaven has brought you here?"

In a few words I explained to him that, having had a quarrel with Shvabrin, I came to ask him—Ivan Ignatitch—to be my second.

Ivan Ignatitch listened to me with great attention, keeping his one eye fixed upon me all the while.

"You wish to say," he said to me, "that you want to kill Shvabrin and that you would like me to be a witness to it? Is that so, may I ask?"

"Exactly so."

"In the name of Heaven, Peter Andreitch, whatever are you thinking of! You have had a quarrel with Shvabrin. What a great misfortune! A quarrel should not be hung round one's neck. He has insulted you, and you have insulted him; he gives you one in the face, and you give him one behind the ear; a second blow from him, another from you—and then each goes his own way; in a little while we bring about a reconciliation... Is it right to kill one's neighbour, may I ask? And suppose that you do kill him—God be with him! I have no particular love for him. But what if he were to let daylight through you? How about the matter in that case? Who would be the worst off then, may I ask?"

The reasonings of the discreet lieutenant produced no effect upon me; I remained firm in my resolution.

"As you please," said Ivan Ignatitch; "do as you like. But why should I be a witness to it? People fight,—what is there wonderful in that, may I ask? Thank Heaven! I have fought against the Swedes and the Turks, and have seen enough of every kind of fighting."

I endeavoured to explain to him, as well as I could, the duty of a second; but Ivan Ignatitch could not understand me at all.

"Have your own way," said he; "but if I ought to mix myself up in the matter at all, it should be to go to Ivan Kouzmitch and report to him, in accordance with the rules of the service, that there was a design on foot to commit a crime within the fortress, contrary to the interest of the crown, and to request him to take the necessary measures—"

I felt alarmed, and implored Ivan Ignatitch not to say anything about the matter to the Commandant; after much difficulty I succeeded in talking him over, he gave me his word, and then I took leave of him.

I spent the evening as usual at the Commandant's house. I endeavoured to appear gay and indifferent, so as not to excite suspicion, and in order to avoid importunate questions; but I confess that I had not that cool assurance which those who find themselves in my position nearly always boast about. That evening I was disposed to be tender and sentimental. Maria Ivanovna pleased me more than usual. The thought that perhaps I was looking at her for the last time, imparted to her in my eyes something touching. Shvabrin likewise put in an appearance. I took him aside and informed him of my interview with Ivan Ignatitch.

"What do we want seconds for?" said he, drily; "we can do without them."

We agreed to fight behind the hayricks which stood near the fortress, and to appear on the ground at seven o'clock the next morning.

We conversed together in such an apparently amicable manner that Ivan Ignatitch was nearly betraying us in the excess of his joy.

"You should have done that long ago," he said to me, with a look of satisfaction; "a bad reconciliation is better than a good quarrel."

"What's that, what's that, Ivan Ignatitch?" said the Commandant's wife, who was playing at cards in a corner. "I did not hear what you said."

Ivan Ignatitch, perceiving signs of dissatisfaction upon my face, and remembering his promise, became confused, and knew not what reply to make. Shvabrin hastened to his assistance.

"Ivan Ignatitch," said he, "approves of our reconciliation."

"And with whom have you been quarrelling, my little father?"

"Peter Andreitch and I have had rather a serious fall out."

"What about?"

"About a mere trifle—about a song, Vassilissa Egorovna."

"A nice thing to quarrel about, a song! But how did it happen?"

"In this way. Peter Andreitch composed a song a short time ago, and this morning he began to sing it to me, and I began to hum my favourite ditty:

'Daughter of the Captain,
'Walk not out at midnight.'

"Then there arose a disagreement. Peter Andreitch grew angry, but then he reflected that everyone likes to sing what pleases him best, and there the matter ended." Shvabrin's insolence nearly made me boil over with fury; but nobody except myself understood his coarse insinuations; at least, nobody paid any attention to them. From songs the conversation turned upon poets, and the Commandant observed that they were all rakes and terrible drunkards, and advised me in a friendly manner to have nothing to do with poetry, as it was contrary to the rules of the service, and would lead to no good.

Shvabrin's presence was insupportable to me. I soon took leave of the Commandant and his family, and returned home. I examined my sword, tried the point of it, and then lay down to sleep, after giving Savelitch orders to wake me at seven o'clock.

The next morning, at the appointed hour, I stood ready behind the hayricks, awaiting my adversary. He soon made his appearance.

"We may be surprised," he said to me, "so we must make haste."

We took off our uniforms, remaining in our waistcoats, and drew our swords. At that moment Ivan Ignatitch and five of the old soldiers suddenly made their appearance from behind a hayrick, and summoned us to go before the Commandant. We obeyed with very great reluctance; the soldiers surrounded us, and we followed behind Ivan Ignatitch, who led the way in triumph, striding along with majestic importance.

We reached the Commandant's house. Ivan Ignatitch threw open the door, exclaiming triumphantly:

"Here they are!" Vassilissa Egorovna came towards us.

"What is the meaning of all this, my dears? A plot to commit murder in our fortress! Ivan Kouzmitch, put them under arrest immediately! Peter Andreitch! Alexei Ivanitch! Give up your swords—give them up at once! Palashka, take the swords into the pantry. Peter Andreitch, I did not expect

*Artist P.P. Sokolov, 19th century*

this of you! Are you not ashamed? As regards Alexei Ivanitch, he was turned out of the Guards for killing a man; he does not believe in God. Do you wish to be like him?"

Ivan Kouzmitch agreed with everything that his wife said, and added:

"Yes, Vassilissa Egorovna speaks the truth; duels are strictly forbidden by the articles of war."

In the meanwhile Palashka had taken our swords and carried them to the pantry. I could not help smiling. Shvabrin preserved his gravity.

"With all due respect to you," he said coldly to her, "I cannot but observe that you give yourself unnecessary trouble in constituting yourself our judge. Leave that to Ivan Kouzmitch; it is his business."

"What do you say, my dear!" exclaimed the Commandant's wife. "Are not husband and wife, then, one soul and one body? Ivan Kouzmitch! what are you staring at? Place them at once in separate corners on bread and water, so that they may be brought to their proper senses, and then let Father Gerasim impose a penance upon them, that they may pray to God for forgiveness, and show themselves repentant before men."

Ivan Kouzmitch knew not what to do. Maria Ivanovna was exceedingly pale. Gradually the storm blew over; the Commandant's wife recovered her composure, and ordered us to embrace each other. Palashka brought back our swords to us. We left the Commandant's house to all appearance perfectly reconciled. Ivan Ignatitch accompanied us.

"Were you not ashamed," I said angrily to him, "to go and report us to the Commandant, after having given me your word that you would not do so?"

"As true as there is a heaven above us, I did not mention a word about the matter to Ivan Kouzmitch," he replied. "Vassilissa Egorovna got everything out of me. She arranged the whole business without the Commandant's knowledge. However, Heaven be thanked that it has all ended in the way that it has!"

With these words he returned home, and Shvabrin and I remained alone.

"Our business cannot end in this manner," I said to him.

"Certainly not," replied Shvabrin; "your blood shall answer for your insolence to me; but we shall doubtless be watched. For a few days, therefore, we must dissemble. Farewell, till we meet again."

And we parted as if nothing were the matter.

Returning to the Commandant's house I seated myself, as usual, near Maria Ivanovna. Ivan Kouzmitch was not at home. Vassilissa Egorovna was occupied with household matters. We were conversing together in an under tone. Maria Ivanovna reproached me tenderly for the uneasiness which I had caused them all by my quarrel with Shvabrin.

"I almost fainted away," said she, "when they told us that you intended to fight with swords. What strange beings men are! For a single word, which they would probably forget a week afterwards, they are ready to murder each other and to sacrifice not only their life, but their conscience and the happiness of those—But I am quite sure that you did not begin the quarrel. Without doubt, Alexei Ivanitch first began it."

"Why do you think so, Maria Ivanovna?"

"Because—he is so sarcastic. I do not like Alexei Ivanitch. He is very disagreeable to me; yet it is strange: I should not like to displease him. That would cause me great uneasiness."

"And what do you think, Maria Ivanovna—do you please him or not?"

Maria Ivanovna blushed and grew confused.

"I think," said she, "I believe that I please him."

"And why do you think so?"

"Because he once proposed to me."

"Proposed! He proposed to you? And when?"

"Last year; two months before your arrival."

"And you refused?"

"As you see. Alexei Ivanitch is, to be sure, a sensible man and of good family, and possesses property; but when I think that I should have to kiss him under the crown[1] in the presence of everybody—no! not for anything in the world!"

Maria Ivanovna's words opened my eyes and explained a great many things. I now understood why Shvabrin calumniated her so remorselessly. He had probably observed our mutual inclination towards each other, and endeavoured to produce a coolness between us. The words which had been the cause of our quarrel appeared to me still more abominable, when, instead of a coarse and indecent jest, I was compelled to look upon them in the light of a deliberate calumny. The wish to chastise the insolent slanderer became still stronger within me, and I waited impatiently for a favourable opportunity for putting it into execution.

I did not wait long. The next day, when I was occupied in composing an elegy, and sat biting my pen while trying to think of a rhyme, Shvabrin tapped at my window. I threw down my pen, took up my sword, and went out to him.

"Why should we delay any longer?" said Shvabrin; "nobody is observing us. Let us go down to the river; there no one will disturb us."

We set out in silence. Descending a winding path, we stopped at the edge of the river and drew our swords. Sh-

---

[1] Crowns are held above the heads of the bride and bridegroom during the marriage ceremony in Russia.

vabrin was more skilful in the use of the weapon than I, but I was stronger and more daring, and Monsieur Beaupré, who had formerly been a soldier, had given me some lessons in fencing which I had turned to good account. Shvabrin had not expected to find in me such a dangerous adversary. For a long time neither of us was able to inflict any injury upon the other; at last, observing that Shvabrin was beginning to relax his endeavours, I commenced to attack him with increased ardour, and almost forced him back into the river. All at once I heard my name pronounced in a loud tone. I looked round and perceived Savelitch hastening down the path towards me… At that same moment I felt a sharp thrust in the breast, beneath the right shoulder, and I fell senseless to the ground.

# Chapter V.
# Love

On recovering consciousness I for some time could neither understand nor remember what had happened to me. I was lying in bed in a strange room, and felt very weak. Before me stood Savelitch with a candle in his hand. Someone was carefully unwinding the bandages which were wrapped round my chest and shoulder. Little by little my thoughts became more collected. I remembered my duel and conjectured that I was wounded. At that moment the door creaked.

"Well, how is he?" whispered a voice which sent a thrill through me.

"Still in the same condition," replied Savelitch with a sigh; "still unconscious, and this makes the fifth day that he has been like it."

I wanted to turn round, but I was unable to do so.

"Where am I? Who is here?" said I with an effort.

Maria Ivanovna approached my bed and leaned over me.

"Well, how do you feel?" said she.

"God be thanked!" replied I in a weak voice. "Is it you, Maria Ivanovna? Tell me—"

I had not the strength to continue and I became silent. Savelitch uttered a shout and his face beamed with delight.

"He has come to himself again! He has come to himself again!" he kept on repeating. "Thanks be to Thee, O Lord! Come, little father, Peter Andreitch! What a fright you have given me! It is no light matter; this is the fifth day—"

Maria Ivanovna interrupted him.

"Do not speak to him too much, Savelitch," said she, "he is still very weak."

She went out of the room and closed the door very quietly after her. My thoughts became agitated. And so I was in the house of the Commandant; Maria Ivanovna had been to see me. I wanted to ask Savelitch a few questions, but the old man shook his head and stopped his ears. Filled with vexation, I closed my eyes and soon fell asleep.

When I awoke I called Savelitch, but instead of him I saw Maria Ivanovna standing before me; she spoke to me in her angelic voice. I cannot describe the delightful sensation which took possession of me at that moment. I seized her hand, pressed it to my lips, and watered it with my tears. Maria did not withdraw it... and suddenly her lips touched my cheek, and I felt a hot fresh kiss imprinted upon it. A fiery thrill passed through me.

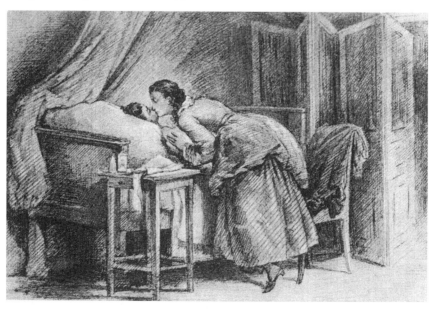

*Artist P.P. Sokolov, 19th century*

"Dear, good Maria Ivanovna," I said to her, "be my wife, consent to make me happy."

She recovered herself.

"For Heaven's sake, calm yourself," said she, withdrawing her hand from my grasp; "you are not yet out of danger: your wound may re-open. Take care of yourself, if only for my sake."

With these words she left the room, leaving me in a transport of bliss. Happiness saved me. "She will be mine! She loves me!" This thought filled my whole being.

From that moment I grew hourly better. The regimental barber attended to the dressing of my wound, for there was no other doctor in the fortress, and, thank heaven, he did not assume any airs of professional wisdom. Youth and nature accelerated my recovery. The whole family of the Commandant attended upon me. Maria Ivanovna scarcely ever left my side. As will naturally be supposed, I seized the first favourable opportunity for renewing my interrupted declaration of love, and this time Maria Ivanovna listened to me more patiently.

Without the least affectation she confessed that she was favourably disposed towards me, and said that her parents, without doubt, would be pleased at her good fortune.

"But think well," she added; "will there not be opposition on the part of your relations?"

This set me thinking. I was not at all uneasy on the score of my mother's affection; but, knowing my father's disposition and way of thinking, I felt that my love would not move him very much, and that he would look upon it as a mere outcome of youthful folly.

I candidly confessed this to Maria Ivanovna, but I resolved, nevertheless, to write to my father as eloquently as possible, to implore his paternal blessing. I showed the letter to Maria Ivanovna, who found it so convincing and touching, that she entertained no doubts about the success of it, and abandoned herself to the feelings of her tender heart with all the confidence of youth and love. With Shvabrin I became reconciled during the first days of my convalescence. Ivan Kouzmitch, reproaching me for having engaged in the duel, said to me:

"See now, Peter Andreitch, I ought really to put you under arrest, but you have been punished enough already without that. As for Alexei Ivanitch, he is confined under guard in the corn magazine, and Vassilissa Egorovna has got his sword under lock and key. He will now have plenty of time to reflect and repent."

I was too happy to cherish any unfriendly feeling in my heart. I began to intercede for Shvabrin, and the good Commandant, with the consent of his wife, agreed to restore him to liberty.

Shvabrin came to me; he expressed deep regret for all that had happened, confessed that he alone was to blame, and begged of me to forget the past. Not being by nature of a rancorous disposition, I readily forgave him the quarrel which he had caused between us, and the wound which I had received at his hands. In his slander I saw nothing but the chagrin of wounded vanity and slighted love, and I generously extended pardon to my unhappy rival.

I soon recovered my health and was able to return to my own quarters. I waited impatiently for a reply to my letter, not daring to hope, and endeavouring to stifle the sad presentiment that was ever uppermost within me. To Vassilissa Egorovna and her husband I had not yet given an explanation; but my proposal would certainly not come as a surprise to them. Neither Maria Ivanovna nor I had endeavoured to hide our feelings from them, and we felt assured of their consent beforehand.

At last, one morning, Savelitch came to me carrying a letter in his hand. I seized it with trembling fingers. The address was in the handwriting of my father. This prepared me for something serious, for the letters I received from home were generally written by my mother, my father merely adding a few lines at the end as a postscript. For a long time I could not make up my mind to break the seal, but kept reading again and again the solemn superscription:

"To my son, Peter Andreitch Grineff,

"Government[1] of Orenburg,

"Fortress of Belogorsk."

I endeavoured to discover from the handwriting the disposition of mind which my father was in when the letter was written. At last I resolved to open it, and I saw at the very first glance that all my hopes were shipwrecked. The letter ran as follows:

"My son Peter,

"Your letter, in which you ask for our paternal blessing and our consent to your marriage with Maria Ivanovna, the daughter of Mironoff, reached us the 15th inst., and not only do I intend to refuse to give you my blessing and my consent, but, furthermore, I intend to come and teach you a lesson for your follies, as I would a child, notwithstanding your officer's rank; for you have shown yourself unworthy to carry the sword which was entrusted to you for the defence of your native country, and not for the purpose of fighting duels with fools like yourself. I shall write at once to Andrei Karlovitch to ask him to transfer you from the fortress of Belogorsk to some place farther away, where you will be cured of your folly. Your mother, on hearing of your duel and your wound, was taken ill through grief, and she is now confined to her bed. I pray to God that He may correct you, although I hardly dare to put my trust in His great goodness.

"Your father — A. G."

The reading of this letter excited within me various feelings. The harsh expressions which my father had so unsparingly indulged in afflicted me deeply. The contempt with which he referred to Maria Ivanovna appeared to me as indecent as it was unjust. The thought of my being transferred from the fortress of Belogorsk to some other military station

---

[1] For administrative purposes Russia was divided into seventy two governments, exclusive of Finland, which enjoyed a separate administration.

terrified me, but that which grieved me more than every-thing else was the intelligence of my mother's illness. I was very much displeased with Savelitch, not doubting that my parents had obtained information of my duel through him. After pacing up and down my narrow room for some time, I stopped before him and said, as I looked frowningly at him:

"It seems that you are not satisfied that, thanks to you, I should be wounded and for a whole month lie at the door of death, but you wish to kill my mother also."

Savelitch gazed at me as if he were thunderstruck.

"In the name of Heaven, master," said he, almost sob-bing, "what do you mean? I the cause of your being wound-ed! God knows that I was running to screen you with my own breast from the sword of Alexei Ivanovitch! My ac-cursed old age prevented me from doing so. But what have I done to your mother?"

"What have you done?" replied I. "Who asked you to write and denounce me? Have you then been placed near me to act as a spy upon me?"

"I write and denounce you?" replied Savelitch, with tears in his eyes. "O Lord, King of Heaven! Be pleased to read what my master has written to me—you will then see whether I have denounced you or not."

And with these words he took from his pocket a letter and handed it to me.

It ran as follows:

"You ought to be ashamed of yourself, you old hound, for not having—in spite of my strict injunctions to you to do so—written to me and informed me of the conduct of my son, Peter Andreitch, and leaving it to strangers to acquaint me with his follies. Is it thus that you fulfil your duty and your master's will? I will send you to tend the pigs, you old hound, for concealing the truth and for indulging the young man. On receipt of this, I command you to write back to me without delay, and inform me of the present state of his health, of the exact place of his wound, and whether he has been well attended to."

It was evident that Savelitch was perfectly innocent, and that I had insulted him with my reproaches and suspicions for no reason at all. I asked his pardon; but the old man was inconsolable.

"That I should have lived to come to this!" he kept on repeating; "these are the thanks that I receive from my master. I am an old hound, a keeper of pigs, and I am the cause of your being wounded. No, little father, Peter Andreitch, it is not I, but that accursed mossoo who is to blame: it was he who taught you to thrust with those iron spits and to stamp your foot, as if by thrusting and stamping one could protect himself from a bad man. It was very necessary to engage that mossoo and so throw good money to the winds!"

But who then had taken upon himself the trouble to denounce my conduct to my father? The general? But he did not appear to trouble himself in the least about me; and Ivan Kouzmitch had not considered it necessary to report my duel to him. I became lost in conjecture. My suspicions settled upon Shvabrin. He alone could derive any advantage from the denunciation, the result of which might be my removal from the fortress and separation from the Commandant's family. I went to inform Maria Ivanovna of everything. She met me on the steps leading up to the door.

"What has happened to you?" said she, on seeing me; "how pale you are!"

"It is all over," replied I, and I gave her my father's letter.

She now grew pale in her turn. Having read the letter, she returned it to me with a trembling hand, and said, with a quivering voice:

"Fate ordains that I should not be your wife... Your parents will not receive me into their family. God's will be done! God knows better than we do, what is good for us. There is nothing to be done, Peter Andreitch; may you be happy—"

"It shall not be!" I exclaimed, seizing hold of her hand. "You love me; I am prepared for everything. Let us go and throw ourselves at the feet of your parents; they are simple people, not hard-hearted and proud. They will give us their blessing; we will get married... and then, with time, I feel quite certain that we shall succeed in bringing my father round; my mother will be on our side; he will forgive me—"

"No, Peter Andreitch," replied Masha, "I will not marry you without the blessing of your parents. Without their blessing you will not be happy. Let us submit to the will of God. If you meet with somebody else, if you love another—God be with you, Peter Andreitch, I will pray for you both—"

Then she burst into tears and left me. I wanted to follow her into her room, but I felt that I was not in a condition to control myself, and I returned home to my quarters.

I was sitting down, absorbed in profound thoughtfulness, when Savelitch interrupted my meditations.

"Here, sir," said he, handing me a written sheet of paper: "see whether I am a spy upon my master, and whether I try to cause trouble between father and son."

I took the paper out of his hand. It was the reply of Savelitch to the letter which he had received. Here it is, word for word:

"Lord Andrei Petrovitch, our gracious father,

"I have received your gracious letter, in which you are pleased to be angry with me, your slave, telling me that I ought to be ashamed of myself for not fulfilling my master's orders. I am not an old hound, but your faithful servant, and I do obey my master's orders, and I have always served you zealously till my grey hairs. I did not write anything to you about Peter Andreitch's wound, in order that I might not alarm you without a reason, and now I hear that our lady, our mother, Avdotia Vassilevna, is ill from fright, and I am going to pray to God to restore her to health. Peter Andreitch was wounded under the right shoulder, in the breast, exactly under a rib, to the depth of nearly three inches, and he was put to bed in the Commandant's house, whither we

*Artist P.P. Sokolov, 19th century*

carried him from the bank of the river, and he was healed by Stepan Paramonoff, the barber of this place, and now, thank God, Peter Andreitch is well, and I have nothing but good to write about him. His superior officers, I hear, are satisfied with him; and Vassilissa Egorovna treats him as if he were her own son. And because such an accident occurred to him, the young man ought not to be reproached: the horse has four legs, and yet he stumbles. And if it please you to write that I should go and feed the pigs, let your lordly will be done. Herewith I humbly bow down before you.

"Your faithful slave,
"Arkhip Savelitch."

I could not help smiling several times while reading the good old man's letter. I was not in a condition to reply to my father, and Savelitch's letter seemed to me quite sufficient to calm my mother's fears.

From this time my situation changed. Maria Ivanovna scarcely ever spoke to me, nay, she even tried to avoid me. The Commandant's house began to become insupportable to me. Little by little I accustomed myself to remaining at home alone. Vassilissa Egorovna reproached me for it at first, but perceiving my obstinacy, she left me in peace. Ivan Kouzmitch I only saw when the service demanded it; with Shvabrin I rarely came into contact, and then against my will, all the more so because I observed in him a secret enmity towards me, which confirmed me in my suspicions. My life became unbearable to me. I sank into a profound melancholy, which was enhanced by loneliness and inaction. My love grew more intense in my solitude, and became more and more tormenting to me. I lost all pleasure in reading and literature. I grew dejected. I was afraid that I should either go out of my mind or that I should give way to dissipation. But an unexpected event, which exercised an important influence upon my after life, suddenly occurred to give to my soul a powerful and salutary shock.

# Chapter VI.
# Pougatcheff

Before I proceed to write a description of the strange events of which I was a witness, I must say a few words concerning the condition of the government of Orenburg towards the end of the year 1773.

This rich and extensive government was inhabited by hordes of half-savage people, who had only recently acknowledged the sovereignty of the Russian Czars. Their continual revolts, their disinclination to a civilized life and an existence regulated by laws, their fickleness and cruelty, demanded on the part of the government a constant vigilance in order to keep them in subjection. Fortresses had been erected in convenient places, and were garrisoned for the most part by Cossacks, who had formerly held possession of the shores of the Yaik. But these Yaikian Cossacks, whose duty it was to preserve peace and to watch over the security of this district, had themselves for some time past become very troublesome and dangerous to the government. In the year 1772 an insurrection broke out in their principal city. The causes of it were the severe measures taken by General Traubenberg to bring the army into a state of obedience. The result was the barbarous murder of Traubenberg, the selection of new leaders, and finally the suppression of the revolt by grapeshot and cruel punishments.

This happened a little while before my arrival at the fortress of Belogorsk. All was now quiet, or at least appeared so; but the authorities believed too easily in the pretended repentance of the cunning rebels, who nursed their hatred in secret and only waited for a favourable opportunity to recommence the struggle. I now return to my narrative.

One evening (it was in the beginning of October in the year 1773) I was sitting indoors alone, listening to the moaning of the autumn wind, and gazing out of the window at the clouds, as they sailed rapidly over the face of the moon. A message was brought to me to wait upon the Commandant. I immediately repaired to his quarters. I there found Shvabrin, Ivan Ignatitch, and the Cossack orderly. Neither Vassilissa Egorovna nor Maria Ivanovna was in the room. The Commandant greeted me with a preoccupied air. He closed the door, made us all sit down except the orderly, who remained standing near the door, drew a paper out of his pocket, and said to us:

"Gentlemen, we have here important news! Hear what the general writes."

Then he put on his spectacles and read as follows:

"To the Commandant of the Fortress of Belogorsk, Captain Mironoff. (*Confidential.*)

"I hereby inform you that the fugitive and schismatic Don Cossack, Emelian Pougatcheff, after having been guilty of the unpardonable insolence of assuming the name of the deceased Emperor Peter III, has collected a band of evil-disposed persons, has excited disturbances in the settlements along the banks of the Yaik, and has already taken and destroyed several fortresses, pillaging and murdering on every side. Therefore, on the receipt of this letter, you, Captain, will at once take the necessary measures to repel the above-mentioned villain and impostor, and, if possible, to completely annihilate him, if he should turn his arms against the fortress entrusted to your care."

"Take the necessary measures," said the Commandant, taking off his spectacles and folding up the letter; "you see that it is very easy to say that. The villain is evidently strong in numbers, whereas we have but 130 men altogether, not counting the Cossacks, upon whom we can place very little dependence—without intending any reproach to you, Maximitch." The orderly smiled. "Still, there is no help for it, but to do the best we can, gentlemen. Let us be on our guard and establish night patrols; in case of attack, shut the gates and assemble the soldiers. You, Maximitch, keep a strict eye on your Cossacks. See that the cannon be examined and thoroughly cleaned. Above all things, keep what I have said a secret, so that nobody in the fortress may know anything before the time."

After giving these orders, Ivan Kouzmitch dismissed us. I walked away with Shvabrin, reflecting upon what we had heard.

"How do you think that this will end?" I asked him.

"God knows," he replied; "we shall see. I do not see anything to be alarmed about at present. If, however—"

Then he began to reflect and to whistle abstractedly a French air.

In spite of all our precautions, the news of the appearance of Pougatcheff soon spread through the fortress. Although Ivan Kouzmitch entertained the greatest respect for his wife, he would not for anything in the world have confided to her a secret entrusted to him in connection with the service. After having received the general's letter, he contrived in a tolerably dexterous manner to get Vassilissa Egorovna out of the way, telling her that Father Gerasim had received some extraordinary news from Orenburg, which he kept a great secret. Vassilissa Egorovna immediately wished to go and pay a visit to the pope's wife and, by the advice of Ivan Kouzmitch, she took Masha with her, lest she should feel dull by herself.

Ivan Kouzmitch, being thus left sole master of the situation, immediately sent for us, having locked Palashka in the pantry, so that she might not be able to overhear what we had to say.

Vassilissa Egorovna returned home, without having succeeded in getting anything out of the pope's wife, and she learned that, during her absence, a council of war had been held in Ivan Kouzmitch's house, and that Palashka had been under lock and key. She suspected that she had been duped by her husband, and she began to assail him with questions. But Ivan Kouzmitch was prepared for the attack. He was not in the least perturbed, and boldly made answer to his inquisitive consort:

"Hark you, mother dear, our women hereabouts have taken a notion into their heads to heat their ovens with straw, and as some misfortune might be the outcome of it, I gave strict orders that the women should not heat their ovens with straw, but should burn brushwood and branches of trees instead."

"But why did you lock up Palashka, then?" asked his wife. "Why was the poor girl compelled to sit in the kitchen till we returned?"

Ivan Kouzmitch was not prepared for such a question; he became confused, and stammered out something very incoherent. Vassilissa Egorovna perceived her husband's perfidy, but, knowing that she would get nothing out of him just then, she abstained from asking any further questions and turned the conversation to the subject of the pickled cucumbers, which Akoulina Pamphilovna knew how to prepare in such an excellent manner. But all that night Vassilissa Egorovna could not sleep a wink, nor could she understand what it was that was in her husband's head that she was not permitted to know.

The next day, as she was returning home from mass, she saw Ivan Ignatitch, who was busily engaged in clearing the cannon of pieces of rag, small stones, bits of bone, and rubbish of every sort, which had been deposited there by the little boys of the place.

"What mean these warlike preparations?" thought the Commandant's wife. "Can it be that they fear an attack on the part of the Kirghises? But is it possible that Ivan Kouzmitch could conceal such a trifle from me?"

She called Ivan Ignatitch to her with the firm determination of learning from him the secret which tormented her woman's curiosity.

Vassillissa Egorovna began by making a few observations to him about household matters, like a judge who commences an examination with questions foreign to the matter in hand in order to lull the suspicions of the person accused. Then after a silence of a few moments, she heaved a deep sigh, and said, shaking her head:

*Artist P.P. Sokolov, 19th century*

"Oh, Lord God! What news! What will be the end of all this?"

"Well, well, mother!" replied Ivan Ignatitch; "God is merciful; we have soldiers enough, plenty of powder and I have cleaned the cannon. Perhaps we shall be able to offer a successful resistance to this Pougatcheff; if God will only not abandon us, we shall be safe enough here."

"And what sort of a man is this Pougatcheff?" asked the Commandant's wife.

Then Ivan Ignatitch perceived that he had said more

than he ought to have done, and he bit his tongue. But it was now too late. Vassilissa Egorovna compelled him to inform her of everything, having given him her word that she would not mention the matter to anybody.

Vassilissa Egorovna kept her promise and said not a word to anybody, except to the pope's wife, and to her only because her cow was still feeding upon the steppe, and might be captured by the brigands.

Soon everybody was talking about Pougatcheff. The (reports concerning him varied very much. The Commandant sent his orderly to glean as much information as possible about him in all the neighbouring villages and fortresses. The orderly returned after an absence of two days, and reported that, at about sixty versts from the fortress, he had seen a large number of fires upon the steppe, and that he had heard from the Bashkirs that an immense force was advancing. He could not say anything more positive, because he had feared to venture further.

An unusual agitation now began to be observed among the Cossacks of the fortress; in all the streets they congregated in small groups, quietly conversing among themselves, and dispersing whenever they caught sight of a dragoon or any other soldier belonging to the garrison. They were closely watched by spies. Youlai, a converted Calmuck, made an important communication to the commandant. The orderly's report, according to Youlai, was a false one; on his return the treacherous Cossack announced to his companions that he had been among the rebels, and had been presented to their leader, who had given him his hand and had conversed with him for a long time. The Commandant immediately placed the orderly under arrest, and appointed Youlai in his place. This change was the cause of manifest dissatisfaction among the Cossacks. They murmured loudly, and Ivan Ignatitch, who executed the Commandant's instructions, with his own ears heard them say:

"Just wait a little while, you garrison rat!"

The Commandant had intended interrogating the prisoner that very same day, but the orderly had made his escape, no doubt with the assistance of his partisans.

A fresh event served to increase the Commandant's uneasiness. A Bashkir, carrying seditious letters, was seized. On this occasion the Commandant again decided upon assembling his officers, and therefore he wished once more to get Vassilissa Egorovna out of the way under some plausible pretext. But as Ivan Kouzmitch was a most upright and sincere man, he could find no other method than that employed on the previous occasion.

"Listen, Vassilissa Egorovna," he said to her, coughing to conceal his embarrassment: "they say that Father Gerasim has received—"

"That's enough, Ivan Kouzmitch," said his wife, interrupting him: "you wish to assemble a council of war to talk about Emelian Pougatcheff without my being present; but you shall not deceive me this time."

Ivan Kouzmitch opened his eyes.

"Well, little mother," he said, "if you know everything, you may remain; we shall speak in your presence."

"Very well, my little father," replied she; "you should not try to be so cunning; send for the officers."

We assembled again. Ivan Kouzmitch, in the presence of his wife, read to us Pougatcheff's proclamation, drawn up probably by some half-educated Cossack. The robber announced therein his intention of immediately marching upon our fortress; he invited the Cossacks and soldiers to join him, and advised the superior officers not to offer any resistance, threatening them with death in the event of their doing so. The proclamation was couched in coarse but vigorous language, and could not but produce a powerful impression upon the minds of simple people.

"What a rascal!" exclaimed the Commandant's wife; "that he should propose such a thing to us. To go out to meet him and lay our flags at his feet! Ah! the son of a dog! He does not know then that we have been forty years in the service, and that, thanks to God, we have seen a good deal during that time. Is it possible that there are commandants who would be cowardly enough to yield to a robber like him?"

"There ought not to be," replied Ivan Kouzmitch; "but it is reported that the scoundrel has already taken several fortresses."

"He seems to have great power," observed Shvabrin. "We shall soon find out the real extent of his power," said the Commandant. "Vassilissa Egorovna, give me the key of the loft. Ivan Ignatitch, bring hither the Bashkir, and tell Youlai to fetch a whip."

"Wait a moment, Ivan Kouzmitch," said his wife, rising from her seat. "Let me take Masha somewhere out of the house; otherwise she will hear the cries and will feel frightened. And I myself, to tell the truth, am no lover of inquisitions. So good-bye for the present."

Torture, in former times, was so rooted in our judicial proceedings, that the benevolent ukase[1] ordering its abolition remained for a long time a dead letter. It was thought that the confession of the criminal was indispensable for his full conviction—an idea not only unreasonable, but even contrary to common sense from a jurisprudential point of view; for if the denial of the accused person be not accepted as proof of his innocence, the confession that has been wrung from him ought still less to be accepted as a proof of his guilt. Even in our days I sometimes hear old judges regretting the abolition of the barbarous custom. But in those days nobody had any doubt about the necessity of torture, neither the judges nor even the accused persons themselves. Therefore it was that the Commandant's order did not astonish or alarm any of us. Ivan Ignatitch went to fetch the Bashkir, who was confined in the loft, under lock and key, and a few minutes afterwards he was led prisoner into the ante-room. The Commandant ordered the captive to be brought before him.

---

[1] Torture was abolished in 1768 by an edict of Catherine II.

The Bashkir stepped with difficulty across the threshold (for his feet were in fetters) and, taking off his high cap, remained standing near the door. I glanced at him and shuddered. Never shall I forget that man. He appeared to be about seventy years of age, and had neither nose nor ears. His head was shaved, and instead of a beard he had a few grey hairs upon his chin; he was of short stature, thin and bent; but his small eyes still flashed fire.

"Ah, ah!" said the Commandant, recognizing by these dreadful marks one of the rebels punished in the year 1741, "I see you are an old wolf; you have already been caught in our traps. It is not the first time that you have rebelled, since your head is planed so smoothly. Come nearer; speak, who sent you here?"

The old Bashkir remained silent and gazed at the Commandant with an air of complete stolidity.

"Why do you not answer?" continued Ivan Kouzmitch. "Don't you understand Russian? Youlai, ask him in your language, who sent him to our fortress."

Youlai repeated the Commandant's question in the Tartar language. But the Bashkir looked at him with the same expression and answered not a word.

"By heaven!" exclaimed the Commandant, "you shall answer me. My lads! take off that ridiculous striped gown of his, and tickle his back. Youlai, see that it is carried out properly."

Two soldiers began to undress the Bashkir. The face of the unhappy man assumed an expression of uneasiness. He looked round on every side, like a poor little animal that has been captured by children. But when one of the soldiers seized his hands to twine them round his neck, and raised the old man upon his shoulders, and Youlai grasped the whip and began to flourish it round his head, then the Bashkir uttered a feeble groan, and, raising his head, opened his mouth, in which, instead of a tongue, moved a short stump.

When I reflect that this happened during my lifetime, and that I now live under the mild government of the Emperor Alexander, I cannot but feel astonished at the rapid progress of civilization, and the diffusion of humane ideas. Young man! if these lines of mine should fall into your hands, remember that those changes which proceed from an amelioration of manners and customs are much better and more lasting than those which are the outcome of acts of violence.

We were all horror-stricken.

"Well," said the Commandant, "it is evident that we shall get nothing out of him. Youlai, lead the Bashkir back to the loft; and let us, gentlemen, have a little further talk about the matter."

We were yet considering our position, when Vassilissa Egorovna suddenly rushed into the room, panting for breath, and beside herself with excitement.

"What has happened to you?" asked the astonished Commandant.

"I have to inform you of a great misfortune!" replied Vassilissa Egorovna. "Nijniosern was taken this morning. Father Gerasim's servant has just returned from there. He saw how they took it. The Commandant and all the officers are hanged, and all the soldiers are taken prisoners. In a little while the villains will be here."

This unexpected intelligence produced a deep impression upon me. The Commandant of the fortress of Nijniosern, a quiet and modest young man, was an acquaintance of mine; two months before he had visited our fortress when on his way from Orenburg along with his young wife, and had stopped for a little while in the house of Ivan Kouzmitch. Nijniosern was about twenty five versts from our fortress. We might therefore expect to be attacked by Pougatcheff at any moment. The fate in store for Maria Ivanovna presented itself vividly to my imagination, and my heart sank within me.

"Listen, Ivan Kouzmitch," said I to the Commandant; "our duty is to defend the fortress to the last gasp; there is no question about that. But we must think about the safety of the women. Send them on to Orenburg, if the road be still open, or to some safer and more distant fortress where these villains will not be able to make their way."

Ivan Kouzmitch turned round to his wife and said to her:

"Listen, mother; would it not be just as well if we sent you away to some place farther off until we have settled matters with these rebels?"

"What nonsense!" said the Commandant's wife. "Where is there a fortress that would be safe from bullets? Why is Belogorsk not safe? Thank God, we have lived in it for two-and-twenty years! We have seen Bashkirs and Kirghises; perhaps we shall also escape the clutches of Pougatcheff."

"Well, mother," replied Ivan Kouzmitch, "stay if you like, if you have such confidence in our fortress. But what shall we do with Masha? All well and good if we offer a successful resistance, or can hold out till we obtain help; but what if the villains should take the fortress?"

"Why, then—"

But at this juncture Vassilissa Egorovna began to stammer and then remained silent, evidently agitated by deep emotion.

"No, Vassilissa Egorovna," continued the Commandant, observing that his words had produced an impression upon her, perhaps for the first time in his life, "Masha must not remain here. Let us send her to Orenburg, to her godmother; there are plenty of soldiers and cannon there, and the walls are of stone. And I would advise you to go there with her; for although you are an old woman, think what might happen to you if the fortress should be taken by storm."

"Very well," replied the Commandant's wife; "let it be so: we will send Masha away. As for me, you need not trouble yourself about asking me to go; I will remain here. Nothing shall make me part from you in my old age to go and seek a lonely grave in a strange country. Together we have lived, together we will die."

"Well, you are right," said the Commandant; "but let us

*Artist P.P. Sokolov, 19th century*

not delay any longer. Go and get Masha ready for the journey. She must set out at daybreak tomorrow, and we shall let her have an escort, although we have not too many men in the fortress to be able to spare any of them. But where is Masha?"

"Along with Akoulina Pamphilovna," replied the Commandant's wife. "She fainted away when she heard of the capture of Nijniosern; I am afraid that she will be ill. Lord God of heaven, what have we lived to see!"

Vassilissa Egorovna went to prepare for her daughter's departure. The consultation with the Commandant was then continued; but I no longer took any part in it, nor did I listen to anything that was said. Maria Ivanovna appeared at supper, her face pale and her eyes red with weeping. We supped in silence, and rose from the table sooner than usual; then taking leave of the family, we all returned to our respective quarters. But I intentionally forgot my sword, and went back for it: I had a presentiment that I should find Maria alone. True enough I met her in the doorway, and she handed me my sword.

"Farewell, Peter Andreitch!" she said to me, with tears in her eyes; "they are going to send me to Orenburg. May you be well and happy. God may be pleased to ordain that we should see each other again if not—"

Here she burst out sobbing. I clasped her in my arms.

"Farewell, my angel!" said I. "Farewell, my darling, my heart's desire! Whatever may happen to me, rest assured that my last thought and last prayer shall be for you."

Masha still continued to weep, resting her head upon my breast. I kissed her fervently, and hastily quitted the room.

# Chapter VII.
# The Assault

That night I neither slept nor undressed. It was my intention to proceed early in the morning to the gate of the fortress through which Maria Ivanovna would have to pass, so that I might take leave of her for the last time. I felt within myself a great change; the agitation of my soul was far less burdensome to me than the melancholy into which I had lately fallen. With the grief of separation there was mingled a vague, but sweet hope, an impatient expectation of danger, a feeling of noble ambition.

The night passed away imperceptibly. I was just about to leave the house when my door opened, and the corporal entered the room with the information that our Cossacks had quitted the fortress during the night, taking Youlai by force along with them, and that strange people were riding round the fortress. The thought that Maria Ivanovna would not be able to get away filled me with alarm. I hurriedly gave some orders to the corporal, and then hastened at once to the Commandant's quarters.

Day had already begun to dawn. I was hurrying along the street when I heard someone call out my name. I stopped.

"Where are you going?" said Ivan Ignatitch, overtaking me. "Ivan Kouzmitch is on the rampart, and he has sent me for you. Pougatch[1] has come."

"Has Maria Ivanovna left the fortress?" I asked, with a trembling heart.

"She was unable to do so," replied Ivan Ignatitch; "the

---

[1] A pun on the name of the rebel chief. Literally, "a scarecrow."

road to Orenburg is cut off and the fortress is surrounded. It is a bad look-out, Peter Andreitch."

We made our way to the rampart, an elevation formed by nature and fortified by a palisade. The inhabitants of the fortress were already assembled there. The garrison stood drawn up under arms. The cannon had been dragged thither the day before. The Commandant was walking up and down in front of his little troop. The approach of danger had inspired the old warrior with unusual vigour. On the steppe, not very far from the fortress, about a score of men could be seen riding about on horseback. They seemed to be Cossacks, but among them were some Bashkirs, who were easily recognized by their hairy caps, and by their quivers.

The Commandant walked along the ranks of his little army, saying to the soldiers:

"Now, my children, let us stand firm today for our mother the Empress,, and let us show the whole world that we are brave people, and true to our oath."

The soldiers responded to his appeal with loud shouts. Shvabrin stood near me and attentively observed the enemy. The people riding about on the steppe, perceiving some movement in the fortress, gathered together in a group and began conversing among themselves. The Commandant ordered Ivan Ignatitch to point the cannon at them, and then applied the match to it with his own hand. The ball whistled over their heads, without doing any harm. The horsemen dispersed, galloping out of sight almost immediately, and the steppe was deserted.

At that moment Vassilissa Egorovna appeared upon the rampart, followed by Masha, who was unwilling to leave her.

"Well," said the Commandant's wife, "how goes the battle? Where is the enemy?"

"The enemy is not far off," replied Ivan Kouzmitch. "God grant that all may go well!... Well, Masha, do you feel afraid?"

"No, papa," replied Maria Ivanovna; "I feel more afraid being at home alone."

Then she looked at me and made an effort to smile. I involuntarily grasped the hilt of my sword, remembering that I had received it from her hand the evening before — as if for the protection of my beloved. My heart throbbed. I imagined myself her champion. I longed to prove that I was worthy of her confidence, and waited impatiently for the decisive moment.

All of a sudden some fresh bodies of mounted men made their appearance from behind an elevation situated about half a mile from the fortress, and soon the steppe was covered with crowds of persons armed with lances and quivers. Among them, upon a white horse, was a man in a red *caftan*,[1] holding a naked sword in his hand; this was Pougatcheff himself. He stopped his horse, and the others gathered round him, and, in obedience to his order as it seemed, four men detached themselves from the crowd and galloped at full speed towards the fortress. We recognized among them some of our traitors. One of them held a sheet of paper above his head, while another bore upon the top of his lance the head of Youlai, which he threw over the palisade among us. The head of the poor Calmuck fell at the feet of the Commandant.

The traitors cried out:

"Do not fire! Come out and pay homage to the Czar. The Czar is here!"

"Look out for yourselves!" cried Ivan Kouzmitch, "Ready, lads — fire!"

Our soldiers fired a volley. The Cossack who held the letter staggered and fell from his horse; the others galloped back. I turned and looked at Maria Ivanovna. Terror-stricken by the sight of the bloodstained head of Youlai, and stunned by the din of the discharge, she seemed perfectly paralyzed. The Commandant called the corporal and ordered him to fetch the paper from the hands of the fallen Cossack. The corporal went out into the plain, and returned leading by

---

[1] A kind of overcoat.

the bridle the horse of the dead man. He handed the letter to the Commandant. Ivan Kouzmitch read it to himself and then tore it into pieces. In the meantime we could see the rebels preparing for the attack. Soon the bullets began to whistle about our ears, and several arrows fell close to us, sticking in the ground and in the palisade.

"Vassilissa Egorovna!" said the Commandant; "women have no business here. Take Masha away; you see that the girl is more dead than alive."

Vassilissa Egorovna, tamed by the bullets, cast a glance at the steppe, where a great commotion was observable, and then turned round to her husband and said to him:

"Ivan Kouzmitch, life and death are in the hands of God; bless Masha. Masha, come near to your father."

Masha, pale and trembling, approached Ivan Kouzmitch knelt down before him, and bowed herself to the ground. The old Commandant made the sign of the cross over her three times, then raised her up, and kissing her, said in a voice of deep emotion:

"Well, Masha, be happy. Pray to God; He will never forsake you. If you find a good man, may God give you love and counsel. Live together as your mother and I have lived. And now, farewell, Masha. Vassilissa Egorovna, take her away quickly."

Masha threw her arms round his neck and sobbed aloud.

"Let us kiss each other also," said the Commandant's wife, weeping. "Farewell, my Ivan Kouzmitch. Forgive me if I have ever vexed you in any way!"

"Farewell, farewell, little mother!" said the Commandant, embracing the partner of his joys and sorrows for so many years. "Come now, that is enough! Make haste home; and if you can manage it, put a sarafan[1] on Masha."

---

[1] A wide open robe without sleeves, beneath which is worn a full long-sleeved gown. It is usually richly embroidered, the embroidery varying according to the rank of the wearer. It was the custom among the Russians to bury the dead in their richest dress.

The Commandant's wife walked away along with her daughter. I followed Maria Ivanovna with my eyes; she turned round and nodded her head to me.

Ivan Kouzmitch then returned to us, and bestowed all his attention upon the enemy. The rebels gathered round their leader and suddenly dismounted from their horses.

"Stand firm now," said the Commandant, "the assault is going to begin."

At that moment frightful yells and cries rose in the air; the rebels dashed forward towards the fortress. Our cannon was loaded with grape-shot.

The Commandant allowed them to come very close, and then suddenly fired again. The grape fell into the very midst of the crowd. The rebels recoiled and then dispersed on every side. Their leader alone remained facing us. He waved his sword and seemed to be vehemently exhorting his followers to return to the attack. The shrieks and yells, which had ceased for a minute, were immediately renewed.

*Artist P.P. Sokolov, 19th century*

"Now, lads!" said the Commandant; "open the gate, seat the drum, and let us make a sally. Forward, and follow me!"

The Commandant, Ivan Ignatitch, and I were outside the wall of the fortress in a twinkling; but the timid garrison did not move.

"Why do you hold back, my children?" cried Ivan Kouzmitch. "If we are to die, let us die doing our duty!"

At that moment the rebels rushed upon us and forced an entrance into the fortress. The drum ceased to beat; the garrison flung down their arms. I was thrown to the ground, but I rose up and entered the fortress along with the rebels. The Commandant, wounded in the head, was surrounded by a crowd of the robbers, who demanded of him the keys. I was about to rush to his assistance, but several powerful Cossacks seized hold of me and bound me with their sashes, exclaiming:

"Just wait a little while and see what you will get, you traitors to the Czar!"

They dragged us through the streets; the inhabitants came out of their houses with bread and salt;[1] the bells began to ring. Suddenly among the crowd a cry was raised that the Czar was in the square waiting for the prisoners to take their oath of allegiance to him. The throng pressed towards the marketplace, and our captors dragged us thither also.

Pougatcheff was seated in an armchair on the steps of the Commandant's house. He was attired in an elegant Cossack *caftan*, ornamented with lace. A tall cap of sable, with gold tassels, came right down to his flashing eyes. His face seemed familiar to me. He was surrounded by the Cossack chiefs. Father Gerasim, pale and trembling, stood upon the steps with a cross in his hands, and seemed to be silently imploring mercy for the victims brought forward. In the square a gallows was being hastily erected. As we approached, the Bashkirs drove back the crowd, and we were brought before Pougatcheff. The bells had ceased ringing, and a deep silence reigned around.

---

[1] The customary offering to a Russian emperor on entering a town.

79

"Which is the Commandant?" asked the pretender.

Our orderly stepped forward out of the crowd and pointed to Ivan Kouzmitch.

Pougatcheff regarded the old man with a menacing look, and said to him:

"How dared you oppose me—your emperor?" The Commandant, weakened by his wound, summoned all his remaining strength and replied in a firm voice:

"You are not my emperor; you are a robber and a pretender, that is what you are!"

*Artist V.G. Perov, 1879*

Pougatcheff frowned savagely and waved his white handkerchief. Several Cossacks seized the old captain and dragged him towards the gallows. Astride upon the cross-beam could be seen the mutilated Bashkir whom we had examined the day before. He held in his hand a rope, and a minute afterwards I saw poor Ivan Kouzmitch suspended in the air. Then Ivan Ignatitch was brought before Pougatcheff. "Take the oath of fealty," said Pougatcheff to him, "to the Emperor Peter Fedorovitch!"

"You are not our emperor, replied Ivan Ignatitch, repeating the words of his captain; "you, uncle, are a robber and a pretender!"

Pougatcheff again waved his handkerchief, and the good lieutenant was soon hanging near his old chief. It was now my turn. I looked defiantly at Pougatcheff, prepared to repeat the answer of my brave comrades, when, to my inexpressible astonishment, I perceived, among the rebels, Shvabrin, his hair cut close, and wearing a Cossack *caftan.* He stepped up to Pougatcheff and whispered a few words in his ear.

"Let him be hanged!" said Pougatcheff, without even looking at me.

The rope was thrown round my neck. I began to repeat a prayer to myself, expressing sincere repentance for all my sins, and imploring God to save all those who were dear to me. I was led beneath the gibbet.

"Don't be afraid, don't be afraid," said my executioners, wishing sincerely, perhaps, to encourage me.

Suddenly I heard a cry:

"Stop, villains! hold!"

The executioners paused. I looked round. Savelitch was on his knees at the feet of Pougatcheff.

"Oh, my father!" said my poor servant; "why should you wish for the death of this noble child? Let him go you will get a good ransom for him; if you want to make an example of somebody for the sake of terrifying others order me to be hanged—an old man!"

Pougatcheff gave a sign, and I was immediately unbound and set at liberty.

"Our father pardons you," said the rebels who had charge of me.

I cannot say that at that moment I rejoiced at my deliverance, neither will I say that I was sorry for it. My feelings were too confused. I was again led before the usurper and compelled to kneel down in front of him Pougatcheff stretched out to me his sinewy hand.

"Kiss his hand, kiss his hand!" exclaimed voices of every side of me.

But I would have preferred the most cruel punishment to such contemptible degradation.

"My little father, Peter Andreitch," whispered Savelitch standing behind me and nudging my elbow, "do not be obstinate. What will it cost you? Spit and kiss the brig—pshaw! kiss his hand!"

*Artist P.P. Sokolov, 19th century*

I did not move. Pougatcheff withdrew his hand, saying with a smile:

"His lordship seems bewildered with joy. Lift him up!"

I was raised to my feet and released. I then stood by to observe the continuation of the terrible comedy.

The inhabitants began to take the oath of allegiance. They approached one after another, kissed the crucifix and then bowed to the usurper. Then came the turn of the soldiers of the garrison. The regimental barber, armed with his blunt scissors, cut off their hair. Then, after shaking their heads, they went and kissed the hand of Pougatcheff, who declared them pardoned, and then enrolled them among his followers.

All this lasted for about three hours. At length Pougatcheff rose up from his armchair and descended the steps, accompanied by his chiefs. A white horse, richly caparisoned, was led forward to him. Two Cossacks took hold of him under the arms and assisted him into the saddle. He informed Father Gerasim that he would dine with him. At that moment a woman's scream was heard. Some of the brigands were dragging Vassilissa Egorovna, with her hair dishevelled and her clothes half torn off her body, towards the steps. One of them had already arrayed himself in her gown. The others were carrying off beds, chests, tea-services, linen, and all kinds of furniture.

"My fathers!" cried the poor old woman, "have pity upon me and let me go. Kind fathers! take me to Ivan Kouzmitch."

Suddenly she caught sight of the gibbet and recognized her husband.

"Villains!" she cried, almost beside herself; "what have you done to him? My Ivan Kouzmitch! light of my life! brave soldier heart! Neither Prussian bayonets nor Turkish bullets have touched you; not in honourable fight have you yielded up your life; you received your death at the hands of a runaway galley-slave!"

"Make the old witch hold her tongue!" said Pougatcheff.

A young Cossack struck her on the head with his sabre, and she fell dead at the foot of the steps. Pougatcheff rode off; the crowd followed him.

# Chapter VIII.
# An Uninvited Guest

The square was deserted. I remained standing in the same place, unable to collect my thoughts, bewildered as I was by so many terrible emotions.

Uncertainty with respect to the fate of Maria Ivanovna tortured me more than anything else. Where was she? What had become of her? Had she contrived to hide herself? Was her place of refuge safe? Filled with these distracting thoughts, I made my way to the Commandant's house. It was empty. The chairs, tables, and chests were broken, the crockery dashed to pieces, and everything in confusion. I ran up the little staircase which led to Maria's room, and which I now entered for the first time in my life. Her bed had been ransacked by the robbers; the wardrobe was broken open and plundered; the small lamp was still burning before the empty image case.[1] There was also left a small mirror hanging on the partition wall... Where was the mistress of this humble, virginal cell? A terrible thought passed through my mind; I imagined her in the hands of the robbers... My heart sank within me... I wept bitterly, most bitterly, and called aloud the name of my beloved... At that moment I heard a slight noise, and from behind the wardrobe appeared Palasha, pale and trembling.

"Ah, Peter Andreitch!" said she, clasping her hands "What a day! what horrors!"

---

[1] The small wardrobe, with glass doors, in which the sacred images are kept, and which forms a domestic altar.

"And Maria Ivanovna?" I asked impatiently. "What has become of Maria Ivanovna?"

"The young lady is alive," replied Palasha; "she is hiding in the house of Akoulina Pamphilovna."

"With the priest's wife!" I exclaimed in alarm. "My God! Pougatcheff is there!"

I dashed out of the room, and in the twinkling of an eye, I was in the street and hurrying off to the clergyman's house, without devoting the slightest attention to anything else. Shouts, songs, and bursts of laughter resounded from within... Pougatcheff was feasting with his companions. Palasha had followed me thither. I sent her to call out Akoulina Pamphilovna secretly. In about a minute the priest's wife came out to me in the vestibule, with an empty bottle in her hand.

"In Heaven's name! where is Maria Ivanovna?" I asked with indescribable agitation.

"The dear little dove is lying down on my bed behind the partition," replied the priest's wife. "But a terrible misfortune had very nearly happened, Peter Andreitch! Thanks be to God, however, everything has passed off happily. The villain had just sat down to dine, when the poor child uttered a moan!... I felt as if I should have died. He heard it. * Who is that moaning in your room, old woman?'—I bowed myself to the ground, and replied: 'My niece, Czar; she has been lying ill for about a fortnight.'—'And is your niece young?'—'She is young, Czar.'—'Show me your niece then, old woman.' My heart sank within me, but there was no help for it. 'Very well, Czar; but the girl will not have the strength to get up and come before your Grace.'—'Never mind, old woman, I will go and see her myself.' And the villain went behind the partition and, will you believe it?— actually drew aside the curtain and looked at her with his hawk-like eyes—but nothing came of it,—God helped us! Will you believe it?

I and the father were prepared for a martyr's death. Fortunately, my little dove did not recognize him. Lord

God! what have we lived to see! Poor Ivan Kouzmitch! who would have thought it!... And Vassilissa Egorovna? And Ivan Ignatitch? What was he killed for? And how came they to spare you? And what do you think of Shvabrin? He has had his hair cut, and is now feasting inside along with them! He is a very sharp fellow, there is no gainsaying that! When I spoke of my sick niece—will you believe it?—he looked at me as if he would have stabbed me; but he did not betray me. I am thankful to him for that, anyway."

At that moment I heard the drunken shouts of the guests and the voice of Father Gerasim. The guests were demanding wine, and the host was calling for his wife. "Go back home, Peter Andreitch," said the priest's wife, somewhat alarmed; "I cannot stop to speak to you now; I must go and wait upon the drunken scoundrels. It might be unfortunate for you if you fell into their hands. Farewell, Peter Andreitch. What is to be, will be; perhaps God will not abandon us!"

The priest's wife went back inside the house. Somewhat more easy in mind, I returned to my quarters. As I crossed the square I saw several Bashkirs assembled round the gibbets, engaged in dragging off the boots of those who had been hanged. With difficulty I repressed my indignation, feeling convinced that if I gave expression to it, it would have been perfectly useless. The brigands invaded every part of the fortress, and plundered the officers' houses. On every side resounded the shouts of the drunken mutineers. I reached home. Savelitch met me on the threshold.

"Thank God!" he exclaimed when he saw me; "I was beginning to think that the villains had seized you again. Ah! my little father, Peter Andreitch, will you believe it, the robbers have plundered us of everything—clothes, linen, furniture, plate—they have not left us a single thing. But what does it matter? Thank God! they have spared your life. But, my lord, did you recognize their leader?"

"No, I did not recognize him. Who is he then?"

"How, my little father! Have you forgotten that drunken scoundrel who swindled you out of the pelisse at the inn? A brand new hare-skin pelisse; and the beast burst the seams in putting it on."

I was astounded. In truth, the resemblance of Pougatcheff to my guide was very striking. I felt convinced that Pougatcheff and he were one and the same person, and then I understood why he had spared my life. I could not but feel surprised at the strange connection of events—a child's pelisse, given to a roving vagrant, had saved me from the hangman's noose, and a drunkard, who had passed his life in wandering from one inn to another, was now besieging fortresses and shaking the empire!

"Will you not eat something?" asked Savelitch, still faithful to his old habits. "There is nothing in the house; but I will go and search, and get something ready for you."

When I was left alone, I began to reflect. What was I to do? To remain in the fortress now that it was in the hands of the villain, or to join his band, was unworthy of an officer. Duty demanded that I should go wherever my services might still be of use to my fatherland in the present critical position of its affairs... But love strongly urged me to remain near Maria Ivanovna and be her protector and defender. Although I foresaw a speedy and inevitable change in the course of affairs, yet I could not help trembling when I thought of the danger of her situation.

My reflections were interrupted by the arrival of one of the Cossacks, who came to inform me that "the great Czar required me to appear before him."

"Where is he?" I asked, preparing to obey.

"In the Commandant's house," replied the Cossack. "After dinner our father took a bath, but at present he is resting. Ah! your Excellency, it is very evident that he is a distinguished person; at dinner he deigned to eat two roasted sucking pigs, then he entered the bath, where the water was so hot that even Tarass Kourotchkin could not bear it; he had to give the besom to Tomka Bikbaieff, and only came to himself through having cold water poured over him. There is no denying it; all his ways are majestic... And I was told that in the bath he showed his Czar's signs upon his breast: on one side a two-headed eagle as large as a five-copeck piece, and on the other his own likeness."

I did not consider it necessary to contradict the Cossack's statement, and I accompanied him to the Commandant's house, trying to imagine beforehand what kind of a reception I should meet with from Pougatcheff, and endeavouring to guess how it would end. The reader will easily understand that I did not by any means feel easy within myself.

It was beginning to get dark when I reached the Commandant's house. The gibbet, with its victims, loomed black and terrible before me. The body of the poor Commandant's wife still lay at the bottom of the steps, near which two Cossacks stood on guard. The Cossack who accompanied me went in to announce me, and, returning almost immediately, conducted me into the room where, the evening before, I had taken a tender farewell of Maria Ivanovna.

An unusual spectacle presented itself to my gaze. At a table, covered with a cloth and loaded with bottles and glasses, sat Pougatcheff and some half-a-score of Cossack chiefs, in coloured caps and shirts, heated with wine, with flushed faces and flashing eyes. I did not see among then Shvabrin and his fellow traitor, the orderly.

"Ah! your Excellency!" said Pougatcheff, seeing me "Welcome; honour to you and a place at our banquet."

The guests moved closer together. I sat down silently at the end of the table. My neighbour, a young Cossack, tall and handsome, poured out for me a glass of wine, which, however, I did not touch. I began to observe the company with curiosity. Pougatcheff occupied the seat of honour, his elbows resting on the table, and his broad fist propped under his black beard. His features, regular and sufficiently agreeable, had nothing fierce about them. He frequently turned to speak to a man of about fifty years of age, addressing him sometimes as Count, sometimes as Timofeitch, sometimes as uncle. All those present treated each other as comrades, and did not show any particular respect for their leader. The conversation was upon the subject of the assault of the morning, of the success of the revolt, and of their future operations. Each one boasted of what he had done, expressed his opinion, and fearlessly contradicted Pougatcheff. And in this strange council of war it was resolved to march upon Orenburg; a bold movement, and which was to be very nearly crowned with success! The march was fixed for the following day.

*Artist P.P. Sokolov, 19th century*

"Now, lads," said Pougatcheff, "before we retire to rest, let us have my favourite song. Choumakoff, begin!"

My neighbour sang, in a shrill voice, the following melancholy peasants' song, and all joined in the chorus:

"Stir not, mother, green forest of oak,
Disturb me not in my meditation;
For tomorrow before the court I must go,
Before the stern judge, before the Czar himself.
The great Lord Czar will begin to question me:

'Tell me, young man, tell me, thou peasant's son,
With whom have you stolen, with whom have you robbed?
Did you have many companions with you?'
'I will tell you, true-believing Czar,
The whole truth I will confess to you.
My companions were four in number:
My first companion was the dark night,
My second companion was a steel knife,
My third companion was my good horse,
My fourth companion was my taut bow,
My messengers were my tempered arrows.'
Then speaks my hope, the true-believing Czar:
'Well done! my lad, brave peasant's son;
You knew how to steal, you knew how to reply:
Therefore, my lad, I will make you a present
Of a very high structure in the midst of a field —
Of two upright posts with a cross-beam above.'"

It is impossible to describe the effect produced upon me by this popular gallows song, trolled out by men destined for the gallows. Their ferocious countenances, their sonorous voices, and the melancholy expression which they imparted to the words, which in themselves were not very expressive, filled me with a sort of poetical terror. The guests drank another glass, then rose from the table and took leave of Pougatcheff.

I wanted to follow them, but Pougatcheff said to me:

"Sit down; I want to speak to you."

We remained face to face.

For some moments we both continued silent. Pougatcheff looked at me fixedly, every now and then winking his left eye with a curious expression of craftiness and drollery. At last he burst out laughing, and with such unfeigned merriment, that I, too, looking at him, began to laugh, without knowing why.

"Well, your lordship," he said to me, "confess now, you were in a terrible fright when my fellows put the rope round your neck. I do not believe that the sky appeared bigger than a sheepskin to you just then... You would have been strung up to the crossbeam if it had not been for your servant. I knew the old fellow at once. Well, would your lordship have thought that the man who conducted you to the inn, was the great Czar himself?"

Here he assumed an air of mystery and importance.

"You have been guilty of a serious offence against me," continued he, "but I pardoned you on account of your virtue, and because you rendered me a service when I was compelled to hide myself from my enemies. But you will see something very different presently! You will see how I will reward you when I enter into possession of my kingdom! Will you promise to serve me with zeal?"

The rascal's question, and his insolence, appeared to me so amusing, that I could not help smiling.

"Why do you smile?" he asked, frowning. "Perhaps you do not believe that I am the great Czar? Is that so?—answer plainly."

I became confused. To acknowledge a vagabond as emperor was quite out of the question; to do so seemed to me unpardonable cowardice. To tell him to his face that he was an impostor was to expose myself to certain death, and that which I was prepared to say beneath the gibbet before the eyes of the crowd, in the first outburst of my indignation, appeared to me now a useless boast. I hesitated. In gloomy silence Pougatcheff awaited my reply. At last (and even now I remember that moment with self-satisfaction) the sentiment of duty triumphed over my human weakness. I replied to Pougatcheff:

"Listen, I will tell you the whole truth. Judge yourself: can I acknowledge you as emperor? You, as a sensible man, would know that it would not be saying what I really bought."

"Who am I, then, in your opinion?"

"God only knows; but whoever you may be, you are playing a dangerous game."

Pougatcheff threw a rapid glance at me.

"Then you do not believe," said he, "that I am the Emperor Peter? Well, be it so. But is not success the reward of the bold? Did not Grishka Otrepieff[1] reign in former days? Think of me what you please, but do not leave me. What does it matter to you one way or the other? Whoever is pope is father. Serve me faithfully and truly, and I will make you a field-marshal and a prince. What do you say?"

"No," I replied with firmness. "I am by birth a nobleman; I have taken the oath of fealty to the empress: I cannot serve you. If you really wish me well, send me back to Orenburg."

Pougatcheff reflected. "But if I let you go," said he, "will you at least promise not to serve against me?"

"How can I promise you that?" I replied. "You yourself know that it does not depend upon my own will. If I am ordered to march against you, I must go—there is no help for it. You yourself are now a chief; you demand obedience from your followers. How would it seem, if I refused to serve when my services were needed? My life is in your hands: if you set me free, I will thank you; if you put me to death, God will be your judge; but I have told you the truth."

My frankness struck Pougatcheff.

"Be it so," said he, slapping me upon the shoulder. "One should either punish completely or pardon completely. Go then where you like, and do what you like. Come tomorrow to say good-bye to me, and now go to bed. I feel very drowsy myself."

---

[1] The first false Demetrius, the Perkin Warbeck of Russia. The real Demetrius was the son of Ivan the Terrible (Ivan IV), and is generally believed to have been assassinated by order of Boris Godunoff, a nobleman of Tartar origin, who was afterwards elected Czar. Otrepieff's story was that his physician had pretended to comply with the orders of Boris, but had substituted the son of a serf for him. Being supported in his claims by the Poles, the pretender succeeded in gaining the throne, but his partiality for everything Polish aroused the national jealousy of the Russians, and he was slain by the infuriated populace of Moscow, after a brief reign of one year.

*Artist P.P. Sokolov, 19th century*

I left Pougatcheff and went out into the street. The night was calm and cold. The moon and stars were shining brightly, lighting up the square and the gibbet. In the fortress all was dark and still. Only in the tavern was a light visible, where could be heard the noise of late revellers. I glanced at the pope's house. The shutters and doors were closed. Everything seemed quiet within.

I made my way to my own quarters and found Savelitch grieving about my absence. The news of my being set at liberty filled him with unutterable joy.

"Thanks be to Thee, Almighty God!" said he, making the sign of the cross. "At daybreak tomorrow we will leave the fortress and go wherever God will direct us. I have prepared something for you; eat it, my little father, and then rest yourself till the morning, as if you were in the bosom of Christ."

I followed his advice and, having eaten with a good appetite, I fell asleep upon the bare floor, worn out both in body and mind.

# Chapter IX.
# The Parting

Early next morning I was awakened by the drum. I went to the place of assembly. There Pougatcheff's followers were already drawn up round the gibbet, where the victims of the day before were still hanging. The Cossacks were on horseback, the soldiers were under arms. Flags were waving. Several cannon, among which I recognized our own, were mounted on travelling gun-carriages. All the inhabitants were gathered together there, awaiting the usurper. Before the steps of the Commandant's house a Cossack stood holding by the bridle a magnificent white horse of Kirghis breed. I looked about for the corpse of the Commandant's wife. It had been pushed a little on one side and covered with a mat. At length Pougatcheff came out of the house. The crowd took off their caps. Pougatcheff stood still upon the steps and greeted his followers. One of the chiefs gave him a bag filled with copper coins, and he began to scatter them by handfuls. The crowd commenced scrambling for them with eager cries, and there was no lack of pushing and scuffling in the attempts to get possession of them. Pougatcheff's chief followers assembled round him. Among them stood Shvabrin. Our eyes met; in mine he could read contempt, and he turned away with an expression of genuine hate and affected scorn. Pougatcheff, seeing me among the crowd, nodded his head to me and called me to him.

"Listen," said he to me, "set off at once for Orenburg and tell the governor and all the generals from me, that they may expect me in about a week. Advise them to receive me with filial love and submission; otherwise they shall not escape a terrible punishment. A pleasant journey, your lordship!"

Then turning round to the crowd and pointing to Shvabrin, he said:

"There, children, is your new Commandant. Obey him in everything; he is answerable to me for you and for the fortress."

I heard these words with alarm: Shvabrin being made governor of the fortress, Maria Ivanovna remained in his power! Great God! what would become of her!

Pougatcheff descended the steps. His horse was brought to him. He vaulted nimbly into the saddle, without waiting for the Cossacks, who were going to help him to mount.

At that moment I saw my Savelitch emerge from the midst of the crowd; he approached Pougatcheff and gave him a sheet of paper. I could not imagine what was the meaning of this proceeding on his part.

"What is this?" asked Pougatcheff, with an air of importance.

"Read it, then you will see," replied Savelitch. Pougatcheff took the paper and examined it for a long time with a consequential look.

"Why do you write so illegibly?" said he at last. "Our lucid eyes[1] cannot decipher a word. Where is my chief secretary?"

A young man, in the uniform of a corporal, immediately ran up to Pougatcheff.

"Read it aloud," said the usurper, giving him the paper.

I was exceedingly curious to know what my follower could have written to Pougatcheff about. The chief secretary, in a loud voice, began to spell out as follows:

"Two dressing-gowns, one of linen and one of striped silk, six roubles."

---

[1] An allusion to the customary form of speech on presenting a petition to the Czar: "I strike the earth with my forehead, and present my petition to your lucid eyes."

"What does this mean?" said Pougatcheff, frowning.

"Order him to read on," replied Savelitch coolly.

The chief secretary continued:

"One uniform coat of fine green cloth, seven roubles.

"One pair of white cloth breeches, five roubles.

"Twelve Holland linen shirts with ruffles, ten roubles.

"A chest and tea-service, two roubles and a half..."

"What is all this nonsense?" exclaimed Pougatcheff. "What are these chests and breeches with ruffles to do with me?"

Savelitch cleared his throat and began to explain.

"This, my father, you will please to understand is a list of my master's goods that have been stolen by those scoundrels—"

"What scoundrels?" said Pougatcheff, threateningly.

"I beg your pardon, that was a slip on my part," replied Savelitch. "They were not scoundrels, but your fellows, who have rummaged and plundered everything. Do not be angry: the horse has got four legs, and yet he stumbles. Order him to read to the end."

"Read on to the end," said Pougatcheff.

The secretary continued:

"One chintz counterpane, another of taffety quilted with cotton wool, four roubles.

"A fox-skin pelisse, covered with red flannel, forty roubles.

"Likewise a hare-skin morning-gown, presented to your Grace at the inn on the steppe, fifteen roubles."

"What's that!" exclaimed Pougatcheff, his eyes flashing fire.

I confess that I began to feel alarmed for my poor servant. He was about to enter again into explanations, but Pougatcheff interrupted him.

"How dare you pester me with such nonsense!" he cried, snatching the paper out of the secretary's hands and flinging it in Savelitch's face. "Stupid old man! You have been robbed; what a misfortune! Why, old greybeard, you ought to be eternally praying to God for me and my lads, that you and your master are not hanging yonder along with the other traitors to me... A hare-skin morning-gown! Do you know that I could order you to be flayed alive and have your skin made into a morning-gown?"

"As you please," replied Savelitch; "but I am not a free man, and must be answerable for my lord's goods."

Pougatcheff was evidently in a magnanimous humour. He turned round and rode off without saying another word. Shvabrin and the chiefs followed him. The troops marched out of the fortress in order. The crowd pressed forward to accompany Pougatcheff. I remained in the square alone with Savelitch. My servant held in his hand the list of my things and stood looking at it with an air of deep regret.

Seeing me on such good terms with Pougatcheff, he thought that he might take advantage of the circumstance; but his sage scheme did not succeed. I was on the point of scolding him for his misplaced zeal, but I could not restrain myself from laughing.

"Laugh away, my lord," replied Savelitch: "laugh away; but when the time comes for you to procure a new outfit, we shall see if you will laugh then."

I hastened to the priest's house to see Maria Ivanovna. The priest's wife met me with sad news. During the night Maria Ivanovna had been seized with a violent attack of fever. She lay unconscious and in a delirium. The priest's wife conducted me into her room. I softly approached her bed. The change in her face startled me. She did not recognize me. For a long time I stood beside her without paying any heed either to Father Gerasim or to his good wife, who endeavoured to console me. Gloomy thoughts took possession of me. The condition of the poor defenceless orphan, left alone in the midst of the lawless rebels, as well as my own powerlessness, terrified me. But it was the thought of Shvabrin more than anything else that filled my imagination with alarm. Invested with power by the usurper, and entrusted with the command of the fortress, in which the unhappy girl—the innocent object of his hatred—remained, he was capable of any villainous act. What was I to do? How should I help her? How could I rescue her out of the hands of the brigands? There remained only one way. I resolved to set out immediately for Orenburg, in order to hasten the deliverance of Belogorsk, and, as far as possible, to cooperate in the undertaking. I took leave of the priest and of Akoulina Pamphilovna, recommending to their care her whom I already considered as my wife. I seized the hand of the poor girl and kissed it, bedewing it with my tears.

"Farewell," said the pope's wife to me, accompanying me to the door; "farewell, Peter Andreitch. Perhaps we shall see each other again in happier times. Do not forget us, and write to us often. Poor Maria Ivanovna has nobody now, except you, to console and protect her."

On reaching the square, I stopped for a moment and looked at the gibbet, then, bowing my head before it, I quitted the fortress and took the road to Orenburg, accompanied by Savelitch, who had not left my side.

I was walking on, occupied with my reflections, when suddenly I heard behind me the trampling of horses' feet. Looking round, I saw, galloping out of the fortress, a Cossack, holding a Bashkir horse by the rein and making signs to me from afar. I stopped and soon recognized our orderly. Galloping up to us, he dismounted from his own horse, and giving me the rein of the other, said:

"Your lordship! our father sends you a horse, and a pelisse from his own shoulders." (To the saddle was attached a sheepskin pelisse.) "Moreover," continued the orderly with some hesitation, "he sends you—half-a-rouble—but I have lost it on the road; be generous and pardon me."

Savelitch eyed him askance and growled out:

"You lost it on the road! What is that chinking in your pocket, then, you shameless rascal!"

"What is that chinking in my pocket?" replied the orderly, without being in the least confused. "God be with you, old man! It is a horse's bit, and not half-a-rouble."

"Very well," said I, putting an end to the dispute. "Give my thanks to him who sent you; and as you go back, try and find the lost half-rouble and keep it for drink-money."

"Many thanks, your lordship," replied he, turning his horse round; "I will pray to God for you without ceasing."

With these words he galloped back again, holding one hand to his pocket, and in about a minute he was hidden from sight.

I put on the pelisse and mounted the horse, taking Savelitch up behind me.

"Now do you see, my lord," said the old man, "that I did not give the petition to the rascal in vain? The robber felt ashamed of himself. Although this lean-looking Bashkir jade and this sheepskin pelisse are not worth half of what the rascals stole from us, and what you chose to give him yourself, they may yet be of some use to us; from a vicious dog, even a tuft of hair."

# Chapter X.
# The Siege

On approaching Orenburg, we saw a crowd of convicts, with shaven heads, and with faces disfigured by the hangman's pincers. They were at work on the fortifications, under the direction of the soldiers of the garrison. Some were carrying away in wheel-barrows the earth and refuse which filled the moat, others with shovels were digging up the ground; on the rampart the masons were carrying stones and repairing the walls. The sentinels stopped us at the gate and demanded our passports. As soon as the sergeant heard that I came from Belogorsk, he took me straight to the General's house.

I found him in the garden. He was inspecting the apple-trees, which the autumn winds had stripped of their leaves, and, with the help of an old gardener, was carefully covering them with straw. His face expressed tranquillity, health, and good-nature. He was much pleased to see me, and began questioning me about the terrible events of which I had been an eye-witness. I related everything to him. The old man listened to me with attention, and continued in the meantime to lop off the dry twigs.

"Poor Mironoff!" said he, when I had finished my sad story; "I feel very sorry for him, he was a good officer; and Madame Mironoff was a good woman,—how clever she was at pickling mushrooms! And what has become of Masha, the Captain's daughter?"

I replied that she was still at the fortress in the hands of the pope and his wife.

"That is bad, very bad. Nobody can place any dependence upon the discipline of robbers. What will become of the poor girl?"

I replied that the fortress of Belogorsk was not far off and that, without doubt, his Excellency would not delay in sending thither a detachment of soldiers to deliver the poor inhabitants.

The General shook his head dubiously.

"We shall see, we shall see," said he, "we have plenty of time to talk about that. Do me the pleasure of taking a cup of tea with me: a council of war is to be held at my house this evening. You may be able to give us some trustworthy information concerning this rascal Pougatcheff and his army. And now go and rest yourself for a little while."

I went to the quarter assigned to me, where Savelitch had already installed himself, and where I awaited with impatience the appointed time. The reader will easily imagine that I did not fail to make my appearance at the council which was to have such an influence upon my fate At the appointed hour I repaired to the General's house.

I found with him one of the civil officials of the town, the director of the custom-house, if I remember rightly, a stout, red-faced old man in a silk coat. He began to question me about the fate of Ivan Kouzmitch, whom he called his gossip, and frequently interrupted my discourse with additional questions and moral observations, which, if they did not prove him to be a man well versed in military matters, showed at least that he possessed sagacity and common sense. In the meantime the other persons who had been invited to the council had assembled. When they were all seated, and a cup of tea had been handed round to each, the General entered into a clear and detailed account of the business in question.

"And now, gentlemen," continued he, "we must decide in what way we are to act against the rebels: offensively or defensively? Each of these methods has its advantages and disadvantages. Offensive warfare holds out a greater prospect of a quicker extermination of the enemy; defensive action is safer and less dangerous... Therefore let us commence by putting the question to the vote in legal order, that is, beginning with the youngest in rank. Ensign," continued he, turning to me, "will you please favour us with your opinion?"

I rose, and after having described, in a few words, Pougatcheff and his followers, I expressed my firm opinion that the usurper was not in a position to withstand disciplined troops.

My opinion was received by the civil officials with evident dissatisfaction. They saw in it only the rashness and temerity of a young man. There arose a murmur, and I distinctly heard the word "greenhorn" pronounced in a whisper. The General turned to me and said with a smile: "Ensign, the first voices in councils of war are generally in favour of adopting offensive measures. We will now continue and hear what others have to say. Mr. Counsellor of the College, tell us your opinion." The little old man in the silk coat hastily swallowed his third cup of tea, into which he had poured some rum, and then replied:

"I think, your Excellency, that we ought to act neither offensively nor defensively."

"How, Sir Counsellor?" replied the astonished General. 'Tactics present no other methods of action; offensive action or defensive..."

"Your Excellency, act diplomatically."

"Ah! your idea is a very sensible one. Diplomatic action is allowed by the laws of tactics, and we will profit by your advice. We might offer for the head of the rascal... seventy or even a hundred roubles... out of the secret funds..."

"And then," interrupted the Director of the Customs, "may I become a Kirghis ram, and not a College Counsellor, if these robbers do not deliver up to us their leader, bound hand and foot."

"We will think about it, and speak of it again," replied the General. "But, in any case, we must take military precautions. Gentlemen, give your votes in regular order."

The opinions of all were contrary to mine. All the civil officials expatiated upon the untrustworthiness of the troops, the uncertainty of success, the necessity of being cautious, and the like. All agreed that it was more prudent to remain behind the stone walls of the fortress under the protection of the cannon, than to try the fortune of arms in the open field. At length the General, having heard all their opinions, shook the ashes from his pipe and spoke as follows:

"Gentlemen, I must declare to you that, for my part, I am entirely of the same opinion as the ensign; because this opinion is founded upon sound rules of tactics, which nearly always give the preference to offensive action rather than to defensive."

Then he paused and began to fill his pipe. My vanity triumphed. I cast a proud glance at the civil officials, who were whispering among themselves with looks of displeasure and uneasiness.

"But, gentlemen," continued the General, heaving a deep sigh, and emitting at the same time a thick cloud of tobacco smoke, "I dare not take upon myself such a great responsibility, when it is a question of the safety of the provinces confided to me by Her Imperial Majesty my Most Gracious Sovereign. Therefore it is that I fall in with the views of the majority, who have decided that it is safer and more prudent to await the siege inside the town, and to repel the attack of the enemy by the use of artillery and—if possible—by sallies."

The officials in their turn now glanced at me ironically. The council separated. I could not but deplore the weakness of this estimable soldier, who, contrary to his own conviction, resolved to follow the advice of ignorant and inexperienced persons.

Some days after this memorable council we heard that Pougatcheff, faithful to his promise, was marching on Orenburg. From the lofty walls of the town I observed the army of the rebels. It seemed to me that their numbers had increased since the last assault, of which I had been a witness. They had with them also some pieces of artillery which had been taken by Pougatcheff from the small fortresses that had been conquered by him. Remembering the decision of the council, I foresaw a long incarceration within the walls of Orenburg, and I was almost ready to weep with vexation.

*Ural Cossacks. Artist Vladimirov, 18th century*

I do not intend to describe the siege of Orenburg, which belongs to history and not to family memoirs. I will merely observe that this siege, through want of caution on the part of the local authorities, was a disastrous one for the inhabitants, who had to endure hunger and every possible privation. It can easily be imagined that life in Orenburg was almost unbearable. All awaited in melancholy anxiety the decision of fate; all complained of the famine, which was really terrible. The inhabitants became accustomed to the cannon-balls falling upon their houses; even Pougatcheff's assaults no longer produced any excitement. I was dying of ennui. Time wore on. I received no letters from Belogorsk; All the roads were cut off. Separation from Maria Ivanovna became insupportable to me. Uncertainty with respect to her fate tortured me. My only diversion consisted in making excursions outside the city. Thanks to the kindness of Pougatcheff, I had a good horse, with which I shared my scanty allowance of food, and upon whose back I used to ride out daily beyond the walls and open fire upon Pougatcheff's partisans. In these skirmishes the advantage was generally on the side of the rebels, who had plenty to eat and drink, and possessed good horses. Our miserable cavalry were unable to cope with them. Sometimes our famished infantry made a sally; but the depth of the snow prevented their operations being successful against the flying cavalry of the enemy. The artillery thundered in vain from the summit of the ramparts, and had it been in the field, it could not have advanced on account of our emaciated horses. Such was our style of warfare! And this was what the civil officials of Orenburg called prudence and foresight!

One day, when we had succeeded in dispersing and driving off a tolerably large body of the enemy, I came up with a Cossack who had remained behind his companions, and I was just about to strike him with my Turkish sabre, when he suddenly took off his cap and cried out:

"Good day, Peter Andreitch; how do you do?"

I looked at him and recognized our orderly. I cannot say how delighted I was to see him.

"Good day, Maximitch," said I to him. "How long is it since you left Belogorsk?"

"Not long, Peter Andreitch; I only returned from there yesterday. I have a letter for you."

"Where is it?" cried I, perfectly beside myself with excitement.

"I have it here," replied Maximitch, placing his hand upon his bosom. "I promised Palasha that I would give it to you somehow."

He then gave me a folded paper and immediately galloped off. I opened it and, deeply agitated, read the following lines:

"It has pleased God to deprive me suddenly of both father and mother: I have now on earth neither a relation nor a protector. I therefore turn to you, because I know that you have always wished me well, and that you are ever ready to help others. I pray to God that this letter may reach you in some way! Maximitch has promised to give it to you. Palasha has also heard from Maximitch that he has frequently seen you from a distance in the sorties, and that you do not take the least care of yourself, not thinking about those who pray to God for you in tears. I was ill a long time, and, when I recovered, Alexei Ivanovitch, who commands here in place of my deceased father, compelled Father Gerasim to deliver me up to him, threatening him with Pougatcheff's anger if he refused. I live in our house which is guarded by a sentry. Alexei Ivanovitch wants to compel me to marry him. He says that he saved my life because he did not reveal the deception practised by Akoulina Pamphílovna, who told the rebels that I was her niece. But I would rather die than become the wife of such a man as Alexei Ivanovitch. He treats me very cruelly, and threatens that if I do not change my mind and agree to his proposal, he will conduct me to the rebels' camp, where I shall suffer the same fate as Elizabeth Kharloff.1 I have begged Alexei Ivanovitch to give me time to reflect. He has consented to give me three days longer, and if at the end of that time I do not agree to become his wife, he will show me no further mercy. Oh, Peter Andreitch! you are my only protector; save a poor helpless girl! Implore the General and all the commanders to send us help as soon as possible, and come yourself if you can.

"I remain your poor obedient orphan,

"Maria Mironoff."

The reading of this letter almost drove me out of my mind. I galloped back to the town, spurring my poor horse without mercy. On the way I turned over in my mind one plan and another for the rescue of the poor girl, but I could not come to any definite conclusion. On reaching the town

---

1 A Commandant's daughter, whom Pougatcheff outraged and then put to death.

I immediately repaired to the General's, and presented myself before him without the least delay.

He was walking up and down the room, smoking his meerschaum pipe. On seeing me he stopped. Probably he was struck by my appearance, for he anxiously inquired the reason of my hasty visit.

"Your Excellency," said I to him, "I come to you as I would to my own father: for Heaven's sake, do not refuse my request; the happiness of my whole life depends upon it!"

"What is the matter?" asked the astonished old soldier. "What can I do for you? Speak!"

"Your Excellency, allow me to take a battalion of soldiers and a company of Cossacks to recapture the fortress of Belogorsk."

The General looked at me earnestly, imagining, without doubt, that I had taken leave of my senses — and, for the matter of that, he was not very far out in his supposition.

"How? — what? Recapture the fortress of Belogorsk?" said he at last.

"I will answer for the success of the undertaking," I replied with ardour; "only let me go."

"No, young man," said he, shaking his head. "At such a great distance the enemy would easily cut off your communication with the principal strategical point, and gain a complete victory over you. Communication being cut off…"

I became alarmed when I perceived that he was about to enter upon a military dissertation, and I hastened to interrupt him.

"The daughter of Captain Mironoff has written a letter to me," I said to him; "she asks for help: Shvabrin wants to compel her to become his wife."

"Indeed! Oh, this Shvabrin is a great rascal, and if he should fall into my hands I will order him to be tried within twenty four hours, and we will have him shot on the parapet of the fortress. But in the meantime we must have patience."

"Have patience!" I cried, perfectly beside myself. "But

in the meantime he will force Maria Ivanovna to become his wife!"

"Oh!" exclaimed the General. "But even that would be no great misfortune for her. It would be better for her to become the wife of Shvabrin, he would then take her under his protection; and when we have shot him we will soon find a sweetheart for her, please God. Pretty widows do not remain single long; I mean that a widow finds a husband much quicker than a spinster."

"I would rather die," said I in a passion, "than resign her to Shvabrin."

"Oh, oh!" said the old man, "now I understand. You are evidently in love with Maria Ivanovna, and that alters the case altogether. Poor fellow! But, for all that, I cannot give you a battalion of soldiers and fifty Cossacks.

Such an expedition would be the height of folly, and I cannot take the responsibility of it upon myself."

I cast down my head; despair took possession of me. Suddenly a thought flashed through my mind: what it was, the reader will discover in the following chapter, as the old romance writers used to say.

# Chapter XI.
# The Rebel Encampment

I left the General and hastened to my own quarters. Savelitch received me with his usual admonitions. "What pleasure do you find, my lord, in fighting against drunken robbers? Is that the kind of occupation for a nobleman? All hours are not alike, and you will sacrifice your life for nothing. It would be all well and good if you were fighting against the Turks or the Swedes, but it is a shame to mention the name of the enemy that you are dealing with now."

I interrupted him in his speech by the question:

"How much money have I left?"

"You have a tolerably good sum still left," he replied, with a look of satisfaction. "In spite of their searching and rummaging, I succeeded in hiding it from the robbers."

So saying, he drew from his pocket a long knitted purse, filled with silver pieces.

"Well, Savelitch," said I to him, "give me half of what you have, and keep the rest yourself. I am going to Fortress Belogorsk."

"My little father, Peter Andreitch!" said my good old servant in a trembling voice; "do not tempt God! How can you travel at the present time, when none of the roads are free from the robbers? Have compassion upon your parents, if you have no pity for yourself. Where do you want to go? And why? Wait a little while. The troops will soon be here and will quickly make short work of the robbers. Then you may go in whatever direction you like."

But my resolution was not to be shaken.

"It is too late to reflect," I said to the old man. "I must go, I cannot do otherwise than go. Do not grieve, Savelitch: God is merciful, perhaps we may see each other again. Have no scruples about spending the money, and don't be sparing of it. Buy whatever you require, even though you have to pay three times the value of it. I give this money to you. If in three days I do not return—"

"What are you talking about, my lord?" said Savelitch, interrupting me. "Do you think that I could let you go alone? Do not imagine anything of the kind. If you have resolved to go, I will accompany you, even though it be on foot; I will not leave you. The idea of my sitting down behind a stone wall without you! Do you think then that I have gone out of my mind? Do as you please, my lord, but I will not leave you."

I knew that it was useless to dispute with Savelitch, and I allowed him to prepare for the journey. In half an hour I was seated upon the back of my good horse, while Savelitch was mounted upon a lean and limping jade, which one of the inhabitants of the town had given to him for nothing, not having the means to keep it any longer. We reached the gates of the town; the sentinels allowed us to pass, and we left Orenburg behind us.

It was beginning to grow dark. My road led past the village of Berd, one of Pougatcheff's haunts. The way was covered with snow, but over the whole of the steppe could be seen the footprints of horses, renewed every day. I rode forward at a quick trot. Savelitch could hardly keep pace with me, and kept calling out:

"Not so fast, my lord, for Heaven's sake, not so fast! My accursed hack cannot keep up with your long-legged devil.

Where are you off to in such a hurry? It would be all very well if we were going to a feast, but we are more likely going to run our heads into a noose... Peter Andreitch... little father... Peter Andreitch! Lord God! the child is rushing to destruction!"

We soon caught sight of the fires of Berd glimmering in

the distance. We approached some ravines, which served as natural defences to the hamlet. Savelitch still followed me, and did not cease to utter his plaintive entreaties. I hoped to be able to ride round the village without being observed, when suddenly I perceived through the darkness, straight in front of me, five peasants armed with clubs; it was the advanced guard of Pougatcheff's camp. They challenged us. Not knowing the password, I wanted to ride on without saying anything; but they immediately surrounded me, and one of them seized hold of my horse's bridle. I drew my sword and struck the peasant on the head. His cap saved him, but he staggered and let the reins fall from his hand. The others grew frightened and took to their heels; I seized the opportunity, and, setting spurs to my horse, I galloped off.

The increasing darkness of the night might have saved me from further dangers, but, turning round all at once, I perceived that Savelitch was no longer with me. The poor old man, with his lame horse, had not been able to get clear of the robbers. What was to be done? After waiting a few minutes for him, and feeling convinced that he had been stopped, I turned my horse round to hasten to his assistance. Approaching the ravine, I heard in the distance confused cries, and the voice of my Savelitch. I quickened my pace, and soon found myself in the midst of the peasants who had stopped me a few minutes before. Savelitch was among them. With loud shouts they threw themselves upon me and dragged me from my horse in a twinkling. One of them, apparently the leader of the band, informed us that he was going to conduct us immediately before the Czar. "And our father," added he, "will decide whether you shall be hanged immediately or wait till daylight."

I offered no resistance; Savelitch followed my example, and the sentinels led us away in triumph.

We crossed the ravine and entered the village. In all the huts fires were burning. Noise and shouts resounded on every side. In the streets I met a large number of people;

but nobody observed us in the darkness, and no one recognized in me an officer from Orenburg. We were conducted straight to a cottage which stood at the corner where two streets met. Before the door stood several wine-casks and two pieces of artillery.

"This is the palace," said one of the peasants; "we will announce you at once."

He entered the cottage. I glanced at Savelitch: the old man was making the sign of the cross and muttering his prayers to himself.

I waited a long time; at last the peasant returned and said to me:

"Come inside; our father has given orders for the officer to be brought before him."

I entered the cottage, or the palace, as the peasants called it. It was lighted by two tallow candles, and the walls were covered with gilt paper; otherwise, the benches, the table, the little wash-hand basin suspended by a cord, the towel hanging on a nail, the oven-fork in the corner, the broad shelf loaded with pots—everything was the same as in an ordinary cottage. Pougatcheff was seated under icons, dressed in a red *caftan* and wearing a tall cap, and with his arms set akimbo in a very self-important manner. Around him stood several of his principal followers, with looks of feigned respect and submission upon their faces. It was evident that the news of the arrival of an officer from Orenburg had awakened a great curiosity among the rebels, and that they had prepared to receive me with as much pomp as possible. Pougatcheff recognized me at the first glance. His assumed importance vanished all at once.

"Ah! your lordship!" said he gaily. "How do you do? What, in Heaven's name, has brought you here?"

I replied that I was travelling on my own business, and that his people had stopped me.

"What business?" asked he.

I knew not what to reply. Pougatcheff, supposing that I did not like to explain in the presence of witnesses, turned to his companions and ordered them to go out of the room. All obeyed, except two, who did not stir from their places.

"Speak boldly before them," said Pougatcheff, "I do not hide anything from them."

I glanced stealthily at the impostor's confidants. One of them, a weazen-faced, crooked old man, with a short grey beard, had nothing remarkable about him except a blue rib-and, which he wore across his grey tunic. But never shall I forget his companion. He was a tall, powerful, broad-shouldered man, and seemed to me to be about forty five years of age. A thick red beard, grey piercing eyes, a nose without nostrils, and reddish scars upon his forehead and cheeks, gave to his broad, pock-marked face an indescribable expression. He had on a red shirt, a Kirghis robe, and Cossack trousers. The first, as I learned afterwards, was the runaway corporal Beloborodoff; the other, Afanassy Sokoloff, surnamed Khlopousha,[1] a condemned criminal, who had three times escaped from the mines of Siberia. In spite of the feelings of agitation which so exclusively occupied my mind at that time, the society in the midst of which I so unexpectedly found myself awakened my curiosity in a powerful degree. But Pougatcheff soon recalled me to myself by his question:

"Speak! on what business did you leave Orenburg?"

A strange thought came into my head: it seemed to me that Providence, by conducting me a second time into the presence of Pougatcheff, gave me the opportunity of carrying my project into execution. I determined to take advantage of it, and, without any further reflection, I replied to Pougatcheff's question:

"I was going to the fortress of Belogorsk to rescue an orphan who is oppressed there."

Pougatcheff's eyes sparkled.

"Which of my people dares to oppress the orphan?" cried he. "Were he seven feet high he should not escape my judgment. Speak! who is the culprit?"

---

[1] The name of a celebrated bandit of the 18th century, who for a long offered resistance to the Imperial troops.

"Shvabrin is the culprit," replied I. "He holds captive the young girl whom you saw ill at the priest's house, and wants to force her to marry him."

"I will soon put Shvabrin in his right place," said Pougatcheff fiercely. "He shall learn what it is to oppress my people according to his own will and pleasure. I will have him hanged."

"Allow me to speak a word," said Khlopousha in a hoarse voice. "You were in too great a hurry in appointing Shvabrin to the command of the fortress, and now you are in too great a hurry to hang him. You have already offended the Cossacks by placing a nobleman over them as their chief; do not now alarm the nobles by hanging them at the first accusation."

"They ought neither to be pitied nor favoured," said the little old man with the blue riband. "To hang Shvabrin would be no great misfortune, neither would it be amiss to put this officer through a regular course of questions. Why has he deigned to pay us a visit? If he does not recognize you as Czar, he cannot come to seek justice from you; and if he does recognize you, why has he remained up to the present time in Orenburg along with your enemies? Will you not order him to be conducted to the court-house, and have a fire lit there?[1] It seems to me that his Grace is sent to us from the generals in Orenburg."

The logic of the old rascal seemed to me to be plausible enough. A shudder passed through the whole of my body, when I thought into whose hands I had fallen. Pougatcheff observed my agitation.

"Well, your lordship," said he to me, winking his eyes; "my Field-Marshal, it seems to me, speaks to the point. What do you think?"

Pougatcheff's raillery restored my courage. I calmly replied that I was in his power, and that he could deal with me in whatever way he pleased.

---

[1] For the purpose of torture.

"Good," said Pougatcheff. "Now tell me, in what condition is your town?"

"Thank God!" I replied, "everything is all right."

"All right!" repeated Pougatcheff, "and the people are dying of hunger!"

The impostor spoke the truth; but in accordance with the duty imposed upon me by my oath, I assured him that what he had heard were only idle reports, and that in Orenburg there was a sufficiency of all kinds of provisions.

"You see," observed the little old man, "that he deceives you to your face. All the deserters unanimously declare that famine and sickness are rife in Orenburg, that they are eating carrion there and think themselves fortunate to get it to eat; and yet his Grace assures us that there is plenty of everything there. If you wish to hang Shvabrin, then hang this young fellow on the same gallows, that they may have nothing to reproach each other with."

The words of the accursed old man seemed to produce an effect upon Pougatcheff. Fortunately, Khlopousha began to contradict his companion.

"That will do, Naoumitch," said he to him: "you only think of strangling and hanging. What sort of a hero are you? To look at you, one is puzzled to imagine how your body and soul contrive to hang together. You have one foot in the grave yourself, and you want to kill others. Haven't you enough blood on your conscience?"

"And what sort of a saint are you?" replied Beloborodoff. "Whence this compassion on your side?"

"Without doubt," replied Khlopousha, "I also am a sinner, and this hand"—here he clenched his bony fist and, pushing back his sleeve, disclosed his hairy arm—"and this hand is guilty of having shed Christian blood. But I killed my enemy, and not my guest; on the open highway or in a dark wood, and not in the house, sitting behind the stove; with the axe and club, and not with old woman's chatter."

The old man turned round and muttered the words: "Slit nostrils!"

"What are you muttering, you old greybeard?" cried Khlopousha. "I will give you slit nostrils. Just wait a little, and your turn will come too. Heaven grant that your nose may smell the pincers... In the meantime, take care that I don't pull out your ugly beard by the roots."

"Gentlemen, generals!" said Pougatcheff loftily, "there has been enough of this quarrelling between you. It would be no great misfortune if all the Orenburg dogs were hanging by the heels from the same crossbeam; but it would be a very great misfortune if our own dogs were to begin devouring each other. So now make it up and be friends again."

Khlopousha and Beloborodoff said not a word, but glared furiously at each other. I felt the necessity of changing the subject of a conversation which might end in a very disagreeable manner for me, and turning to Pougatcheff, I said to him with a cheerful look:

"Ah! I had almost forgotten to thank you for the horse and pelisse. Without you I should never have reached the town, and I should have been frozen to death on the road."

My stratagem succeeded. Pougatcheff became good-humoured again.

"The payment of a debt is its beauty," said he, winking his eyes. "And now tell me, what have you to do with this young girl whom Shvabrin persecutes? Has she kindled a flame in your young heart, eh?"

"She is my betrothed," I replied, observing a favourable change in the storm, and not deeming it necessary to conceal the truth.

"Your betrothed!" exclaimed Pougatcheff. "Why did you not say so before? We will marry you, then, and have some merriment at your wedding!" Then turning to Beloborodoff:

"Listen, Field-Marshal!" said he to him: "his lordship and I are old friends; let us sit down to supper; morning's judgment is wiser than that of evening—so we will see to-morrow what is to be done with him."

I would gladly have declined the proposed honour, but

there was no help for it. Two young Cossack girls, daughters of the owner of the cottage, covered the table with a white cloth, and brought in some bread, fish-soup, and several bottles of wine and beer, and for the second time I found myself seated at the same table with Pougatcheff and his terrible companions.

The drunken revel, of which I was an involuntary witness, continued till late into the night. At last, intoxication began to overcome the three associates. Pougatcheff fell off to sleep where he was sitting: his companions rose and made signs to me to leave him where he was. I went out with them. By order of Khlopousha, the sentinel conducted me to the justice-room, where I found Savelitch, and where they left me shut up with him. My servant was so astonished at all he saw and heard, that he could not ask me a single question. He lay down in the dark, and continued to sigh and moan for a long time; but at length he began to snore, and I gave myself up to meditations, which hindered me from obtaining sleep for a single minute during the whole of the night.

The next morning, Pougatcheff gave orders for me to be brought before him. I went to him. In front of his door stood a *kibitka*, with three Tartar horses harnessed to it. The crowd filled the street. I encountered Pougatcheff in the hall. He was dressed for a journey, being attired in a fur cloak and a Kirghis cap. His companions of the night before stood around him, exhibiting an appearance of submission, which contrasted strongly with everything that I had witnessed the previous evening. Pougatcheff saluted me in a cheerful tone, and ordered me to sit down beside him in the *kibitka*.

We took our seats.

"To the fortress of Belogorsk!" said Pougatcheff to the broad-shouldered Tartar who drove the vehicle. My heart beat violently. The horses broke into a gallop, the little bell tinkled, and the *kibitka* flew over the snow.

"Stop! stop!" cried a voice which I knew only too well, and I saw Savelitch running towards us.

*Artist S.V. Ivanov, 1899*

Pougatcheff ordered the driver to stop.

"Little father, Peter Andreitch!" cried my servant; "do not leave me in my old age among these scoun—"

"Ah, old greybeard!" said Pougatcheff to him. "It is God's will that we should meet again. Well, spring up behind."

"Thanks, Czar, thanks, my own father!" replied Savelitch, taking his seat. "May God give you a hundred years of life and good health for deigning to cast your eyes upon and console an old man. I will pray to God for you all the days of my life, and I will never again speak about the hare-skin pelisse."

This allusion to the hare-skin pelisse might have made Pougatcheff seriously angry. Fortunately, the usurper did not hear, or pretended not to hear, the misplaced remark. The horses again broke into a gallop; the people in the streets stood still and made obeisance. Pougatcheff bowed his head from side to side. In about a minute we had left the village behind us and were flying along over the smooth surface of the road.

One can easily imagine what my feelings were at that moment. In a few hours I should again set eyes upon her whom I had already considered as lost to me for ever. I pictured to myself the moment of our meeting... I thought also of the man in whose hands lay my fate, and who, by a strange concourse of circumstances, had become mysteriously connected with me. I remembered the thoughtless cruelty and the bloodthirsty habits of him, who now constituted himself the deliverer of my beloved. Pougatcheff did not know that she was the daughter of Captain Mironoff; the exasperated Shvabrin might reveal everything to him; it was also possible that Pougatcheff might find out the truth in some other way... Then what would become of Maria Ivanovna? A shudder passed through my frame, and my hair stood on end.

Suddenly Pougatcheff interrupted my meditations, by turning to me with the question:

"What is your lordship thinking of?"

"What should I not be thinking of," I replied. "I am an officer and a gentleman; only yesterday I was fighting against you, and now today I am riding side by side with you in the same carriage, and the happiness of my whole life depends upon you."

"How so?" asked Pougatcheff. "Are you afraid?"

I replied that, having already had my life spared by him, I hoped, not only for his mercy, but even for his assistance.

"And you are right; by God, you are right!" said the impostor. "You saw that my fellows looked askant at you; and this morning the old man persisted in his statement that you were a spy, and that it was necessary that you should be interrogated by means of torture and then hanged. But I would not consent to it," he added, lowering his voice, so that Savelitch and the Tartar should not be able to hear him, "because I remembered your glass of wine and hareskin pelisse. You see now that I am not such a bloodthirsty creature as your brethren maintain."

I recalled to mind the capture of the fortress of Belogorsk but I did not think it advisable to contradict him, and so I made no reply.

"What do they say of me in Orenburg?" asked Pougatcheff, after a short interval of silence.

"They say that it will be no easy matter to get the upper hand of you; and there is no denying that you have made yourself felt."

The face of the impostor betokened how much his vanity was gratified by this remark.

"Yes," said he, with a look of self-satisfaction, "I wage war to some purpose. Do you people in Orenburg know about the battle of Youzeiff?[1] Forty general officers killed, Hour armies taken captive. Do you think the King of Prussia could do as well as that?"

The boasting of the brigand appeared to me to be somewhat amusing.

"What do you think about it yourself?" I said to him: "do you think that you could beat Frederick?"

"Fedor Fedorovitch?[2] And why not? I beat your generals, and they have beaten him. My arms have always been successful up till now. But only wait awhile, you will see something very different when I march to Moscow."

"And do you intend marching to Moscow?"

The impostor reflected for a moment and then said in a low voice:

"God knows. My road is narrow; my will is weak. My followers do not obey me. They are scoundrels. I must keep a sharp look-out; at the first reverse they will save their own necks at the expense of my head."

"That is quite true," I said to Pougatcheff. "Would it not be better for you to separate yourself from them in good time, and throw yourself upon the mercy of the Empress?"

Pougatcheff smiled bitterly.

---

[1] An engagement in which Pougatcheff had the advantage.

[2] The name given to Frederick the Great by the Russian soldiers.

"No," replied he: "it is too late for me to repent now. There would be no pardon for me. I will go on as I have begun. Who knows? Perhaps I shall be successful. Grishka Otrepieff was made Czar at Moscow."

"And do you know what his end was? He was flung out of a window, his body was cut to pieces and burnt, and then his ashes were placed in a cannon and scattered to the winds!"

"Listen," said Pougatcheff with a certain wild inspiration.

"I will tell you a tale which was told to me in my childhood by an old Calmuck. 'The eagle once said to the crow: "Tell me, crow, why is it that you live in this bright world for three hundred years, and I only for thirty three years?" — "Because, little father," replied the crow, "you drink live blood, and I live on carrion." —The eagle reflected for a little while and then said: "Let us both try and live on the same food." — "Good! agreed!" The eagle and the crow flew away. Suddenly they caught sight of a fallen horse, and they alighted upon it. The crow began to pick its flesh and found it very good. The eagle tasted it once, then a second time, then shook its pinions and said to the crow: "No, brother crow; rather than live on carrion for three hundred years, I would prefer to drink live blood but once, and trust in God for what might happen afterwards!"' What do you think of the Calmuck's story?"

"It is very ingenious," I replied. "But to live by murder and robbery is, in my opinion, nothing else than living on carrion."

Pougatcheff looked at me in astonishment and made no reply. We both became silent, each being wrapped in his own thoughts. The Tartar began to hum a plaintive song. Savelitch, dozing, swayed from side to side. The *kibitka* glided along rapidly over the smooth frozen road... Suddenly I caught sight of a little village on the steep bank of the Yaik, with its palisade and belfry, and about a quarter of an hour afterwards we entered the fortress of Belogorsk.

# Chapter XII.
# The Orphan

The *kibitka* drew up in front of the Commandant's house. The inhabitants had recognized Pougatcheff's little bell, and came crowding around us. Shvabrin met the impostor at the foot of the steps. He was dressed as a Cossack, and had allowed his beard to grow. The traitor helped Pougatcheff to alight from the *kibitka* expressing, in obsequious terms, his joy and zeal. On seeing me, he became confused; but quickly recovering himself, he stretched out his hand to me, saying:

"And are you also one of us? You should have been so long ago!"

I turned away from him and made no reply.

My heart ached when we entered the well-known room, on the wall of which still hung the commission of the late Commandant, as a mournful epitaph of the past. Pougatcheff seated himself upon the same sofa on which Ivan Kouzmitch was accustomed to fall asleep, lulled by the scolding of his wife. Shvabrin himself brought him some brandy. Pougatcheff drank a glass, and said to him, pointing to me:

"Give his lordship a glass."

Shvabrin approached me with his tray, but I turned away from him a second time. He seemed to have become quite another person. With his usual sagacity, he had certainly perceived that Pougatcheff was dissatisfied with him.

He cowered before him, and glanced at me with distrust.

Pougatcheff asked some questions concerning the condition of the fortress, the reports referring to the enemy's army, and the like. Then suddenly and unexpectedly he said to him:

"Tell me, my friend, who is this young girl that you hold a prisoner here? Show her to me." Shvabrin turned as pale as death.

"Czar," said he, in a trembling voice..." Czar, she is not a prisoner... she is ill... she is in bed."

"Lead me to her," said the impostor, rising from his seat.

Refusal was impossible. Shvabrin conducted Pougatcheff to Maria Ivanovna's room. I followed behind them. Shvabrin stopped upon the stairs.

"Czar," said he: "you may demand of me whatever you please; but do not permit a stranger to enter my wife's bedroom."

I shuddered.

"So you are married!" I said to Shvabrin, ready to tear him to pieces.

"Silence!" interrupted Pougatcheff: "that is my business. And you," he continued, turning to Shvabrin, "keep your airs and graces to yourself: whether she be your wife or whether she be not, I will take to her whomsoever I please. Your lordship, follow me."

At the door of the room Shvabrin stopped again, and said in a faltering voice:

"Czar, I must inform you that she is in a high fever, and has been raving incessantly for the last three days."

"Open the door!" said Pougatcheff.

Shvabrin began to search in his pockets and then said that he had not brought the key with him. Pougatcheff pushed the door with his foot; the lock gave way, the door opened, and we entered.

I glanced round the room—and nearly fainted away. On the floor, clad in a ragged peasant's dress, sat Maria Ivanovna, pale, thin, and with dishevelled hair. Before her stood a pitcher of water, covered with a piece of bread. Seeing me, she shuddered and uttered a piercing cry. What I felt at that moment I cannot describe.

Pougatcheff looked at Shvabrin and said with a sarcastic smile: "You have a very nice hospital here!"

Then approaching Maria Ivanovna:

"Tell me, my little dove, why does your husband punish you in this manner?"

"My husband!" repeated she. "He is not my husband. I will never be his wife! I would rather die, and I will die, if I am not set free."

Pougatcheff cast a threatening glance at Shvabrin.

"And you have dared to deceive me!" he said to him. "Do you know, scoundrel, what you deserve?"

Shvabrin fell upon his knees... At that moment contempt extinguished within me all feelings of hatred and resentment. I looked with disgust at the sight of a nobleman grovelling at the feet of a runaway Cossack. Pougatcheff relented.

"I forgive you this time," he said to Shvabrin: "but bear in mind that the next time you are guilty of an offence, I will remember this one also."

Then he turned to Maria Ivanovna and said to her kindly:

"Go, my pretty girl; I give you your liberty. I am the Czar."

Maria Ivanovna glanced rapidly at him, and intuitively divined that before her stood the murderer of her parents. She covered her face with both hands and fainted away. I hastened towards her; but at that moment my old acquaintance, Palasha, very boldly entered the room, and began to attend to her young mistress. Pougatcheff quitted the apartment, and we all three entered the parlour.

"Well, your lordship," said Pougatcheff smiling, "we have set the pretty girl free! What do you say to sending for the pope and making him marry his niece to you? If you like, I will act as father, and Shvabrin shall be your best man. We will then smoke and drink and make ourselves merry to our hearts' content!"

*Artist P.P. Sokolov, 19th century*

What I feared took place. Shvabrin, hearing Pougatcheff's proposal, was beside himself with rage.

"Czar!" he exclaimed, in a transport of passion, "I am guilty; I have lied to you; but Grineff is deceiving you also. This young girl is not the pope's niece: she is the daughter of Ivan Mironoff, who was hanged at the taking of the fortress."

Pougatcheff glanced at me with gleaming eyes.

"What does this mean?" he asked in a gloomy tone.

"Shvabrin has told you the truth," I replied in a firm voice.

"You did not tell me that," replied Pougatcheff, whose face had become clouded.

"Judge of the matter yourself," I replied: "could I, in the presence of your people, declare that she was the daughter of Mironoff? They would have torn her to pieces! Nothing would have saved her!"

"You are right," said Pougatcheff smiling. "My drunkards would not have spared the poor girl; the pope's wife did well to deceive them."

"Listen," I continued, seeing him so well disposed; "I know not what to call you, and I do not wish to know... But God is my witness that I would willingly repay you with my life for what you have done for me. But do not demand of me anything that is against my honour and my Christian conscience. You are my benefactor. End as you have begun: let me go away with that poor orphan wherever God will direct us. And wherever you may be, and whatever may happen to you, we will pray to God every day for the salvation of your soul..."

Pougatcheff's fierce soul seemed touched.

"Be it as you wish!" said he. "Punish thoroughly or pardon thoroughly: that is my way. Take your beautiful one, take her wherever you like, and may God grant you love and counsel!"

Then he turned to Shvabrin and ordered him to give me a safe conduct for all barriers and fortresses subjected to his authority. Shvabrin, completely dumbfounded, stood as if petrified. Pougatcheff then went off to inspect the fortress. Shvabrin accompanied him, and I remained behind under the pretext of making preparations for my departure.

I hastened to Maria's room. The door was locked. I

knocked.

"Who is there?" asked Palasha. I called out my name. The sweet voice of Maria Ivanovna sounded from behind the door:

"Wait a moment, Peter Andreitch. I am changing my dress. Go to Akoulina Pamphilovna; I shall be there presently."

I obeyed and made my way to the house of Father Gerasim. He and his wife came forward to meet me. Savelitch had already informed them of what had happened. "You are welcome, Peter Andreitch," said the pope's wife. "God has ordained that we should meet again. And how are you? Not a day has passed without our talking about you. And Maria Ivanovna, the poor little dove, what has she not suffered while you have been away! But tell us, little father, how did you manage to arrange matters with Pougatcheff? How was it that he did not put you to death? The villain be thanked for that, at all events!"

"Enough, old woman," interrupted Father Gerasim. "Don't babble about everything that you know. There is no salvation for chatterers. Come in, Peter Andreitch, I beg of you. It is a long, long time since we saw each other."

The pope's wife set before me everything that she had in the house, without ceasing to chatter away for a single moment. She related to me in what manner Shvabrin had compelled them to deliver Maria Ivanovna up to him; how the poor girl wept and did not wish to be parted from them: how she had kept up a constant communication with them by means of Palashka[1] (a bold girl who compelled the orderly himself to dance to her pipe); how she had advised Maria Ivanovna to write a letter to me, and so forth.

I then, in my turn, briefly related to them my story. The pope and his wife made the sign of the cross on hearing that Pougatcheff had become acquainted with their deception.

"The power of the Cross defend us!" ejaculated Akouli-

---

[1] Diminutive of Palasha.

na Pamphilovna. "May God grant that the cloud will pass over. Well, well, Alexei Ivanitch, you are a very nice fellow: there is no denying that!"

At that moment the door opened, and Maria Ivanovna entered the room with a smile upon her pale face. She had doffed her peasant's dress, and was attired as before, plainly and becomingly.

I grasped her hand and for some time could not utter a single word. We were both silent from fullness of heart. Our hosts felt that their presence was unnecessary to us, and so they withdrew. We were left by ourselves. Everything else was forgotten. We talked and talked and could not say enough to each other. Maria related to me all that had happened to her since the capture of the fortress; she described to me all the horror of her situation, all the trials which she had experienced at the hands of the detestable Shvabrin. We recalled to mind the happy days of the past, and we could not prevent the tears coming into our eyes. At last I began to explain to her my project. For her to remain in the fortress, subjected to Pougatcheff and commanded by Shvabrin, was impossible. Neither could I think of taking her to Orenburg, just then undergoing all the calamities of a siege. She had not a single relative in the whole world. I proposed to her that she should seek shelter with my parents. She hesitated at first: my father's unfriendly disposition towards her frightened her. I made her mind easy on that score. I knew that my father would consider himself bound in honour to receive into his house the daughter of a brave and deserving soldier who had lost his life in the service of his country.

"Dear Maria Ivanovna," I said at last: "I look upon you as my wife. Strange circumstances have united us together indissolubly; nothing in the world can separate us."

Maria Ivanovna listened to me without any assumption of affectation. She felt that her fate was linked with mine. But she repeated that she would never be my wife, except with the consent of my parents. I did not contradict her. We kissed each other fervently and passionately, and in this manner everything was resolved upon between us. About an hour afterwards, the orderly brought me my safe conduct, inscribed with Pougatcheff's scrawl, and informed me that his master wished to see me. I found him ready to get out on his road. I cannot describe what I felt on taking leave of this terrible man, this outcast, so villainously cruel to all except myself alone. But why should I not tell the truth? At that moment I felt drawn towards him by a powerful sympathy. I ardently wished to tear him away from the midst of the scoundrels, whom he commanded, and save his head while there was yet time. Shvabrin, and the crowd gathered around us, prevented me from giving expression to all that filled my heart.

We parted as friends. Pougatcheff, catching sight of Akoulina Pamphilovna among the crowd, threatened her with his finger and winked significantly; then he seated himself in his *kibitka*, and gave orders to return to Berd; and when the horses started off, he leaned once out of the carriage, and cried out to me: "Farewell, your lordship! Perhaps we shall see each other again!"

We did indeed see each other again, but under what circumstances!

Pougatcheff was gone. I stood for a long time gazing across the white steppe, over which his *troika*[1] went gliding rapidly. The crowd dispersed. Shvabrin disappeared. I returned to the pope's house. Everything was ready for our departure; I did not wish to delay any longer. Our luggage had already been deposited in the Commandant's old travelling carriage. The horses were harnessed in a twinkling. Maria Ivanovna went to pay a farewell visit to the graves of her parents, who were buried behind the church. I wished to accompany her, but she begged of me to, let her go alone. After a few minutes she returned silently weeping. The carriage was ready. Father Gerasim and his wife came out upon the steps. Maria Ivanovna, Palasha and I took our places in-

---

[1] An open vehicle drawn by three horses yoked abreast.

side the *kibitka*, while Savelitch seated himself in the front.

"Farewell, Maria Ivanovna, my little dove; farewell, Peter Andreitch, my fine falcon!" said the pope's good wife. "A safe journey, and may God bless you both and make you happy!"

We drove off. At the window of the Commandant's house I perceived Shvabrin standing. His face wore an expression of gloomy malignity. I did not wish to triumph over a defeated enemy, so I turned my eyes the other way.

At last we passed out of the gate, and left the fortress of Belogorsk behind us for ever.

# Chapter XIII.
# The Arrest

United so unexpectedly with the dear girl, about whom I was so terribly uneasy that very morning, I could scarcely believe the evidence of my senses, and imagined that everything that had happened to me was nothing but an empty dream. Maria Ivanovna gazed thoughtfully, now at me, now at the road, and seemed as if she had not yet succeeded in recovering her senses. We were both silent. Our hearts were too full of emotion. The time passed almost imperceptibly, and after journeying for about two hours, we reached the next fortress, which was also subject to Pougatcheff. Here we changed horses. By the rapidity with which this was effected, and by the obliging manner of the bearded Cossack who had been appointed Commandant by Pougatcheff, I perceived that, thanks to the gossip of our driver, I was taken for a favourite of their master.

We continued our journey. It began to grow dark. We approached a small town, where, according to the bearded Commandant, there was a strong detachment on its way to join the impostor. We were stopped by the sentries. In answer to the challenge: "Who goes there?" our driver replied in a loud voice: "The Czar's friend with his little wife."

Suddenly a troop of hussars surrounded us, uttering the most terrible curses.

"Step down, friend of the devil!" said a moustached sergeant-major. "We will make it warm for you and your little wife!"

I got out of the *kibitka* and requested to be brought before their commander. On seeing my officer's uniform, the soldiers ceased their imprecations, and the sergeant conducted me to the major.

Savelitch followed me, muttering:

"So much for your being a friend of the Czar! Out of the frying-pan into the fire. Lord Almighty! how is all this going to end?"

The *kibitku* followed behind us at a slow pace. In about five minutes we arrived at a small, well-lighted house. The sergeant-major left me under a guard and entered to announce me. He returned immediately and informed me that his Highness had no time to receive me, but that he had ordered that I should be taken to prison, and my wife conducted into his presence.

"What does this mean?" I exclaimed in a rage. "Has he taken leave of his senses?"

"I do not know, your lordship," replied the sergeant-major. "Only his Highness has ordered that your lordship should be taken to prison, and her ladyship conducted into his presence, your lordship!"

I dashed up the steps. The sentinel did not think of detaining me, and I made my way straight into the room, where six hussar officers were playing at cards. The major was dealing. What was my astonishment when, looking at him attentively, I recognized Ivan Ivanovitch Zourin, who had once beaten me at play in the Simbirsk tavern.

"Is it possible?" I exclaimed. "Ivan Ivanovitch! Is it really you?"

"Zounds! Peter Andreitch! What chance has brought you here? Where have you come from? How is it with you, brother? Won't you join in a game of cards?"

"Thank you, but I would much rather you give orders for quarters to be assigned to me."

"What sort of quarters do you want? Stay with me."

"I cannot: I am not alone."

"Well, bring your comrade with you."

"I have no comrade with me; I am with a—lady."

"A lady! Where did you pick her up? Aha, brother mine!"

And with these words, Zourin whistled so significantly that all the others burst out laughing, and I felt perfectly confused.

"Well," continued Zourin: "let it be so. You shall have quarters. But it is a pity... We should have had one of our old sprees... I say, boy! Why don't you bring in Pougatcheff's lady friend? Or is she obstinate? Tell her that she need not be afraid, that the gentleman is very kind and will do her no harm—then bring her in by the collar."

"What do you mean?" said I to Zourin. "What lady-friend of Pougatcheff's are you talking of? It is the daughter of the late Captain Mironoff. I have released her from captivity, and I am now conducting her to my father's country seat, where I am going to leave her."

"What! Was it you then who was announced to me just now? In the name of Heaven! what does all this mean?"

"I will tell you later on. For the present, I beg of you to set at ease the mind of this poor girl, who has been terribly frightened by your hussars."

Zourin immediately issued the necessary orders. He went out himself into the street to apologize to Maria Ivanovna for the involuntary misunderstanding, and ordered the sergeant-major to conduct her to the best lodging in the town. I remained to spend the night with him.

We had supper, and when we two were left together, I related to him my adventures. Zourin listened to me with the greatest attention. When I had finished, he shook his head, and said:

"That is all very well, brother; but there is one thing which is not so; why the devil do you want to get married? As an officer and a man of honour, I do not wish to deceive you; but, believe me, marriage is all nonsense. Why should you saddle yourself with a wife and be compelled to dandle children? Scout the idea. Listen to me: shake off this Captain's daughter. I have cleared the road to Simbirsk, and it is quite safe. Send her tomorrow by herself to your parents, and you remain with my detachment. There is no need for you to return to Orenburg. If you should again fall into the hands of the rebels, you may not escape from them so easily a second time. In this way your love folly will die a natural death, and everything will end satisfactorily."

Although I did not altogether agree with him, yet I felt that duty and honour demanded my presence in the army of the Empress. I resolved to follow Zourin's advice: to send Maria Ivanovna to my father's estate, and to remain with his detachment.

Savelitch came in to help me to undress; I told him that he was to get ready the next day to accompany Maria Ivanovna on her journey. He began to make excuses.

"What do you say, my lord? How can I leave you? Who will look after you? What will your parents say?"

Knowing the obstinate disposition of my follower, I resolved to get round him by wheedling and coaxing him.

"My dear friend, Arkhip Savelitch!" I said to him: "do not refuse me; be my benefactor. I do not require a servant here, and I should not feel easy if Maria Ivanovna were to set out on her journey without you. By serving her you will be serving me, for I am firmly resolved to marry her, as soon as circumstances will permit."

Here Savelitch clasped his hands with an indescribable look of astonishment.

"To marry!" he repeated: "the child wants to marry! But what will your father say? And your mother, what will she think?"

"They will give their consent, without a doubt, when they know Maria Ivanovna," I replied. "I count upon you. My father and mother have great confidence in you; you will therefore intercede for us, won't you?"

The old man was touched.

"Oh, my father, Peter Andreitch!" he replied, "although you are thinking of getting married a little too early, yet Maria Ivanovna is such a good young lady, that it would be a pity to let the opportunity escape. I will do as you wish. I will accompany her, the angel, and I will humbly say to your parents, that such a bride does not need a dowry."

I thanked Savelitch, and then lay down to sleep in the same room with Zourin. Feeling very much excited, I began to chatter. At first Zourin listened to my remarks very willingly; but little by little his words became rarer and more disconnected, and at last, instead of replying to one of my questions, he began to snore. I stopped talking and soon followed his example.

The next morning I betook myself to Maria Ivanovna. I communicated to her my plans. She recognized the reasonableness of them, and immediately agreed to carry them out. Zourin's detachment was to leave the town that day. There was no time to be lost. I at once took leave of Maria Ivanovna, confiding her to the care of Savelitch, and giving her a letter to my parents.

Maria burst into tears.

"Farewell, Peter Andreitch," said she in a gentle voice. "God alone knows whether we shall ever see each other again or not; but I will never forget you; till my dying day you alone shall live in my heart!"

I was unable to reply. There was a crowd of people around us, and I did not wish to give way to my feelings before them. At last she departed. I returned to Zourin, silent and depressed. He endeavoured to cheer me up, and I tried to divert my thoughts; we spent the day in noisy mirth, and in the evening we set out on our march.

It was now near the end of February. The winter, which had rendered all military movements extremely difficult, was drawing to its close, and our generals began to make preparations for combined action. Pougatcheff was still under the walls of Orenburg, but our divisions united and began to close in from every side upon the rebel camp. On the appearance of our troops, the revolted villages returned to their allegiance; the rebel bands everywhere retreated before us, and everything gave promise of a speedy and successful termination to the campaign.

Soon afterwards Prince Golitzin defeated Pougatcheff under the walls of the fortress of Tatischtscheff, routed his troops, relieved Orenburg, and to all appearances seemed to have given the final and decisive blow to the rebellion.

*Emelian Pougatcheff. Unknown artist of 18th century*

Zourin was sent at this time against a band of rebellious Bashkirs, who, however, dispersed before we were able to come up with them. The spring found us in a little Tartar village. The rivers overflowed their banks, and the roads became impassable. We consoled ourselves for our inaction with the thought that there would soon be an end to this tedious petty warfare with brigands and savages.

But Pougatcheff was not yet taken. He soon made his appearance in the manufacturing districts of Siberia, where he collected new bands of followers and once more commenced his marauding expeditions. Reports of fresh successes on his part were soon in circulation. We heard of the destruction of several Siberian fortresses. Then came the news of the capture of Kazan, and the march of the impostor to Moscow, which greatly disturbed the leaders of the army, who had fondly imagined that the power of the despised rebel had been completely broken. Zourin received orders to cross the Volga.

I will not describe our march and the conclusion of the war. I will only say that the campaign was as calamitous as it possibly could be. Law and order came to an end everywhere, and the land-holders concealed themselves in the woods. Bands of robbers scoured the country in all directions; the commanders of isolated detachments punished and pardoned as they pleased; and the condition of the extensive territory in which the conflagration raged, was terrible… Heaven grant that we may never see such a senseless and merciless revolt again!

Pougatcheff took to flight, pursued by Ivan Ivanovitch Michelson. We soon heard of his complete overthrow. At last Zourin received news of the capture of the impostor, and, at the same time, orders to halt. The war was ended. At last it was possible for me to return to my parents. The thought of embracing them, and of seeing Maria Ivanovna again, of whom I had received no information, filled me with delight. I danced about like a child. Zourin laughed and said with a shrug of his shoulders:

"No good will come of it! If you get married, you are lost!"

In the meantime a strange feeling poisoned my joy: the thought of that evil-doer, covered with the blood of so many innocent victims, and of the punishment that awaited him, troubled me involuntarily.

"Emelia, Emelia!"[1] I said to myself with vexation, "why did you not dash yourself against the bayonets, or fall beneath the bullets? That was the best thing you could have done."[2]

And how could I feel otherwise? The thought of him was inseparably connected with the thought of the mercy which he had shown to me in one of the most terrible moments of my life, and with the deliverance of my bride from the hands of the detested Shvabrin. Zourin granted me leave of absence. In a few days' time I should again be in the midst of my family, and should once again set eyes upon the face of my Maria Ivanovna... Suddenly an unexpected storm burst upon me.

On the day of my departure, and at the very moment when I was preparing to set out, Zourin came to my hut, holding in his hand a paper, and looking exceedingly troubled. A pang went through my heart. I felt alarmed, without knowing why. He sent my servant out of the room, and said that he had something to tell me.

"What is it?" I asked with uneasiness. "Something rather disagreeable," replied he, giving me the paper. "Read what I have just received." I read it: it was a secret order to all the commanders of detachments to arrest me wherever I might be found, and to send me without delay under a strong guard to Kazan, to appear before the Commission instituted for the trial of Pougatcheff.

The paper nearly fell from my hands. "There is no help for it," said Zourin, "my duty is to obey orders. Probably the report of your intimacy with Pougatcheff has in some way reached the ears of the authorities. I hope that the affair will have no serious consequences, and that you will be able to

---

[1] Diminutive of Emelian.

[2] After having advanced to the gates of Moscow, Pougatcheff was defeated, and being afterwards sold by his accomplices for 100,000 roubles, he was imprisoned in an iron cage and carried to Moscow, where he was executed in the year 1775.

justify yourself before the Commission. Keep up your spirits and set out at once."

My conscience was clear, and I did not fear having to appear before the tribunal; but the thought that the hour of my meeting with Maria might be deferred for several months, filled me with misgivings.

The *telega*[1] was ready. Zourin took a friendly leave of me, and I took my place in the vehicle. Two hussars with drawn swords seated themselves, one on each side of me, and we set out for our destination.

---

[1] An open vehicle without springs.

# Chapter XIV.
# The Sentence

I felt convinced that the cause of my arrest was my absenting myself from Orenburg without leave. I could easily justify myself on that score: for sallying out against the enemy had not only not been prohibited, but had even been encouraged. I might be accused of undue rashness instead of disobedience of orders. But my friendly intercourse with Pougatcheff could be proved by several witnesses, and could not but at least appear very suspicious. During the whole of the journey I thought of the examination that awaited me, and mentally prepared the answers that I should make. I resolved to tell the plain unvarnished truth before the court, feeling convinced that this was the simplest and, at the same time, the surest way of justifying myself.

I arrived at Kazan—the town had been plundered and set on fire. In the streets, instead of houses, there were to be seen heaps of burnt stones, and blackened walls without roofs or windows. Such were the traces left by Pougatcheff! I was conducted to the fortress which had escaped the ravages of the fire. The hussars delivered me over to the officer of the guard. The latter ordered a blacksmith to be sent for. Chains were placed round my feet and fastened together. Then I was taken to the prison and left alone in a dark and narrow dungeon, with four blank walls and a small window protected by iron gratings.

Such a beginning boded no good to me. For all that, I did not lose hope nor courage. I had recourse to the consolation of all those in affliction, and after having tasted for the first time the sweet comforting of prayer poured out from a pure but sorrow-stricken heart, I went off into a calm sleep, without thinking of what might happen to me.

The next morning the gaoler awoke me with the announcement that I was to appear before the Commission. Two soldiers conducted me through a courtyard to the Commandant's house: they stopped in the ante-room and allowed me to enter the inner room by myself.

I found myself in a good-sized apartment. At the table, which was covered with papers, sat two men: an elderly general, of a cold and stern aspect, and a young captain of the Guards, of about twenty eight years of age, and of very agreeable and affable appearance. Near the window, at a separate table, sat the secretary, with a pen behind his ear, and bending over his paper, ready to write down my depositions.

The examination began. I was asked my name and profession. The General inquired if I was the son of Andrei Petrovitch Grineff, and on my replying in the affirmative, he exclaimed in a stern tone:

"It is a pity that such an honourable man should have such an unworthy son!"

I calmly replied that whatever were the accusations against me, I hoped to be able to refute them by the candid avowal of the truth.

My assurance did not please him.

"You are very audacious, my friend," said he, frowning: "but we have dealt with others like you."

Then the young officer asked me under what circumstances and at what time I had entered Pougatcheff's service, and in what affairs I had been employed by him.

I replied indignantly, that, as an officer and a nobleman,

I could never have entered Pougatcheff's service, and could never have received any commission from him whatever.

"How comes it then," continued the interrogator, "that the nobleman and officer was the only one spared by the impostor, while all his comrades were cruelly murdered? How comes it that this same officer and nobleman could revel with the rebellious scoundrels, and receive from the leader of the villains presents, consisting of a pelisse, a horse, and half a rouble? Whence came such strange friendship, and upon what does it rest, if not upon treason, or at least upon abominable and unpardonable cowardice?"

I was deeply offended by the words of the officer of the Guards, and I began to defend myself with great warmth.

I related how my acquaintance with Pougatcheff began upon the steppe during a snow-storm, how he had recognized me at the capture of the fortress of Belogorsk and spared my life. I admitted that I had received a pelisse and a horse from the impostor, but that I had defended the fortress of Belogorsk against the rebels to the last extremity. In conclusion I appealed to my General, who could bear witness to my zeal during the disastrous siege of Orenburg.

The stern old man took up from the table an open letter and began to read it aloud:

"In reply to your Excellency's inquiry respecting Ensign Grineff, who is charged with being implicated in the present insurrection and with entering into communication with the leader of the robbers, contrary to the rules of the service and the oath of allegiance, I have the honour to report that the said Ensign Grineff formed part of the garrison in Orenburg from the beginning of October 1773 to the twenty fourth of February of the present year, on which date he quitted the town, and since that time he has not made his appearance again. We have heard from some deserters that he was in Pougatcheff's camp, and that he accompanied him to the fortress of Belogorsk, where he had formerly been garrisoned. With respect to his conduct, I can only..."

Here the General interrupted his reading and said to me harshly:

"What do you say now by way of justification?"

I was about to continue as I began and explain the state of affairs between myself and Maria Ivanovna as frankly as all the rest, but suddenly I felt an invincible disgust at the thought of doing so. It occurred to my mind, that if I mentioned her name, the Commission would summon her to appear, and the thought of connecting her name with the vile doings of hardened villains, and of herself being confronted with them—this terrible idea produced such an impression upon me, that I became confused and maintained silence.

My judges, who seemed at first to have listened to my answers with a certain amount of good-will, were once more prejudiced against me on perceiving my confusion The officer of the Guards demanded that I should be confronted with my principal accuser. The General ordered that the "rascal of yesterday" should be summoned. I turned round quickly towards the door, to await the appearance of my accuser. After a few moments I heard the clanking of chains, the door opened, and—Shvabrin entered the room. I was astonished at the change in his appearance. He was terribly thin and pale. His hair, but a short time ago as black as pitch, was now quite grey; his long beard was unkempt. He repeated all his accusations in a weak but determined voice. According to his account, I had been sent by Pougatcheff to Orenburg as a spy; every day I used to ride out to the advanced posts, in order to transmit written information of all that took place within the town; that at last I had gone quite over to the side of the usurper and had accompanied him from fortress to fortress, endeavouring in every way to injure my companions in crime, in order to occupy their places and profit the better by the rewards of the impostor.

I listened to him in silence, and I rejoiced on account of one thing: the name of Maria was not mentioned by the scoundrel, whether it was that his self-love could not bear the thought of one who had rejected him with contempt, or that within his heart there was a spark of that self-same feeling which had induced me to remain silent. Whatever it was, the name of the daughter of the Commandant of Belogorsk was not pronounced in the presence of the Commission. I became still more confirmed in my resolution, and when the judges asked me what I had to say in answer to Shvabrin's evidence, I replied that I still stood by my first statement and that I had nothing else to add in justification of myself.

The General ordered us to be led away. We quitted the room together. I looked calmly at Shvabrin, but did not say a word to him. He looked at me with a malicious smile, lifted up his fetters and passed out quickly in front of me. I was conducted back to prison, and was not compelled to undergo a second examination.

I was not a witness of all that now remains for me to impart to the reader; but I have heard it related so often, that the most minute details are indelibly engraven upon my memory, and it seems to me as if I had taken a part in them unseen.

*Artist P.P. Sokolov, 19th century*

Maria Ivanovna was received by my parents with that sincere kindness which distinguished people in the olden time. They regarded it as a favour from God that the opportunity was afforded them of sheltering and consoling the poor orphan. They soon became sincerely attached to her, because it was impossible to know her and not to love her. My love for her no longer appeared mere folly to my father, and my mother had one wish only, that her Peter should marry the pretty Captain's daughter.

The news of my arrest filled all my family with consternation. Maria Ivanovna had related so simply to my parents my strange acquaintance with Pougatcheff, that not only had they felt quite easy about the matter, but had often been obliged to laugh heartily at the whole story. My father would not believe that I could be implicated in an infamous rebellion, the aim of which was the destruction of the throne and the extermination of the nobles. He questioned Savelitch severely. My retainer did not deny that I had been the guest of Pougatcheff, and that the villain had acted very generously towards me, but he affirmed with a solemn oath that he had never heard a word about treason. My old parents became easier in mind, and waited impatiently for more favourable news. Maria Ivanovna, however, was in a state of great agitation, but she kept silent, as she was modest and prudent in the highest degree.

Several weeks passed... Then my father unexpectedly received from St. Petersburg a letter from our relative, Prince B—. The letter was about me. After the usual compliments, he informed him that the suspicions which had been raised concerning my participation in the plots of the rebels, had unfortunately been shown to be only too well founded; that capital punishment would have been meted out to me, but that the Empress, in consideration of the faithful services and the grey hairs of my father, had resolved to be gracious towards his criminal son, and, instead of condemning him to suffer an ignominious death, had ordered that he should be sent to the most remote part of Siberia for the rest of his life.

This unexpected blow nearly killed my father. He lost his usual firmness, and his grief, usually silent, found vent in bitter complaints.

"What!" he cried, as if beside himself: "my son has taken part in Pougatcheff's plots! God of Justice, that I should live to see this! The Empress spares his life! Does that make it any better for me? It is not death at the hands of the executioner that is so terrible: my great grandfather died upon the scaffold for the defence of that which his conscience regarded as sacred; my father suffered with Volinsky and Khroushcheff.[1] But that a nobleman should be false to his oath, should associate with robbers, with murderers and with runaway slaves!... Shame and disgrace upon our race!"

Frightened by his despair, my mother dared not weep in his presence; she endeavoured to console him by speaking of the uncertainty of reports, and the little dependency to be placed upon the opinions of other people. But my father was inconsolable.

Maria Ivanovna suffered more than anybody. Being firmly convinced that I could have justified myself if I had only wished to do so, she guessed the reason of my silence, and considered herself the cause of my misfortune. She hid from everyone her tears and sufferings, and was incessantly thinking of the means by which I might be saved.

One evening my father was seated upon the sofa turning over the leaves of the "Court Calendar," but his thoughts were far away, and the reading of the book failed to produce upon him its usual effect. He was whistling an old march. My mother was silently knitting a woollen waistcoat, and from time to time her tears ran down upon her work. All at once, Maria Ivanovna, who was also at work in the same room, declared that it was absolutely necessary that she should go to St. Petersburg, and she begged of my parents to furnish her with the means of doing so. My mother was very much hurt at this resolution.

"Why do you wish to go to St. Petersburg?" said she. "Is it possible, Maria Ivanovna, that you want to forsake us also?"

---

[1] Chiefs of the Russian party against Biron, the unscrupulous German favourite of the Empress Anne.

Maria replied that her fate depended upon this journey, that she was going to seek help and protection from powerful persons, as the daughter of a man who had fallen a victim to his fidelity.

My father lowered his head; every word that recalled to mind the supposed crime of his son, was painful to him, and seemed like a bitter reproach.

"Go, my child," he said to her at last with a sigh; "we do not wish to stand in the way of your happiness. May God give you an honest man for a husband, and not an infamous traitor."

He rose and left the room.

Maria Ivanovna, left alone with my mother, confided to her a part of her plan. My mother, with tears in her eyes, embraced her and prayed to God that her undertaking might be crowned with success. Maria Ivanovna made all her preparations, and a few days afterwards she set out on her road with the faithful Palasha and the equally faithful Savelitch, who, forcibly separated from me, consoled himself at least with the thought that he was serving my betrothed.

Maria Ivanovna arrived safely at Sofia, and learning that the Court was at that time at Tsarskoe Selo, she resolved to stop there. At the post-house, a small recess behind a partition was assigned to her. The postmaster's wife came immediately to chat with her, and she informed Maria that she was niece to one of the stove-lighters of the Court, and she initiated her into all the mysteries of Court life. She told her at what hour the Empress usually got up, when she took coffee, and when she went out for a walk; what great lords were then with her; what she had deigned to say the day before at table, and whom she had received in the evening. In a word, the conversation of Anna Vlassievna was as good as a volume of historical memoirs, and would be very precious to the present generation. Maria Ivanovna listened to her with great attention. They went together into the palace garden. Anna Vlassievna related the history of every alley and of every little bridge, and after seeing all that they wished to see, they returned to the post-house, highly satisfied with each other.

The next day, early in the morning, Maria Ivanovna awoke, dressed herself, and quietly betook herself to the palace garden. It was a lovely morning; the sun was gilding the tops of the linden trees, already turning yellow beneath the cold breath of autumn. The broad lake glittered in the light. The swans, just awake, came sailing majestically out from under the bushes overhanging the banks. Maria Ivanovna walked towards a delightful lawn, where a monument had just been erected in honour of the recent victories gained by Count Peter Alexandrovitch Roumyanzoff.[1] Suddenly a little white dog of English breed ran barking towards her. Maria grew frightened and stood still. At the same moment she heard an agreeable female voice call out:

"Do not be afraid, it will not bite."

Maria saw a lady seated on the bench opposite the monument. Maria sat down on the other end of the bench. The lady looked at her attentively; Maria on her side, by a succession of stolen glances, contrived to examine the stranger from head to foot. She was attired in a white morning gown, a light cap, and a short mantle. She seemed to be about forty years of age. Her face, which was full and red, wore an expression of calmness and dignity, and her blue eyes and smiling lips had an indescribable charm about them. The lady was the first to break silence.

"You are doubtless a stranger here?" said she.

"Yes, I only arrived yesterday from the country."

"Did you come with your parents?"

"No, I came alone."

"Alone! But you are very young to travel alone."

"I have neither father nor mother."

"Perhaps you have come here on some business?"

"Yes, I have come to present a petition to the Empress."

"You are an orphan: probably you have come to com-

---

[1] A famous Russian general who distinguished himself in the war against the Turks.

plain of some injustice."

"No, I have come to ask for mercy, not justice."

"May I ask you who you are?"

"I am the daughter of Captain Mironoff."

"Of Captain Mironoff! the same who was Commandant of one of the Orenburg fortresses?"

"The same, Madam."

The lady appeared moved.

"Forgive me," said she, in a still kinder voice, "for interesting myself in your business; but I am frequently at Court; explain to me the nature of your request, and perhaps I may be able to help you."

Maria Ivanovna arose and thanked her respectfully Everything about this unknown lady drew her towards her and inspired her with confidence. Maria drew from her pocket a folded paper and gave it to her unknown protectress, who read it to herself.

At first she began reading with an attentive and benevolent expression; but suddenly her countenance changed, and Maria, whose eyes followed all her movements, became frightened by the severe expression of that face, which a moment before had been so calm and gracious.

"You are supplicating for Grineff?" said the lady in a cold tone. "The Empress cannot pardon him. He went over to the usurper, not out of ignorance and credulity, but as a depraved and dangerous scoundrel."

"Oh! it is not true!" exclaimed Maria.

"How, not true?" replied the lady, her face flushing.

"It is not true; as God is above us, it is not true! I know all, I will tell you everything. It was for my sake alone that he exposed himself to all the misfortunes that have overtaken him. And if he did not justify himself before the Commission, it was only because he did not wish to implicate me."

She then related with great warmth all that is already known to the reader.

The lady listened to her attentively.

"Where are you staying?" she asked, when Maria

*Catherine II strolling in the park.*
*Artist V.L. Borovikovsky, 1794*

had finished her story; and hearing that it was with Anna Vlassievna, she added with a smile:

"Ah, I know. Farewell; do not speak to anybody about our meeting. I hope that you will not have to wait long for an answer to your letter."

With these words she rose from her seat and proceeded down a covered alley, while Maria Ivanovna returned to Anna Vlassievna, filled with joyful hopes.

Her hostess scolded her for going out so early; the autumn air, she said, was not good for a young girl's health. She brought an urn, and over a cup of tea she was about to begin her endless discourse about the Court, when suddenly a carriage with armorial bearings stopped before the door, and a lackey entered with the announcement that the Empress summoned to her presence the daughter of Captain Mironoff.

Anna Vlassievna was perfectly amazed.

"Good Lord!" she exclaimed: "the Empress summons you to Court. How did she get to know anything about you? And how will you present yourself before Her Majesty, my little mother? I do not think that you even know how to walk according to Court manners… Shall I conduct you? I could at any rate give you a little caution. And how can you go in your travelling dress? Shall I send to the nurse for her yellow gown?"

The lackey announced that it was the Empress's pleasure that Maria Ivanovna should go alone and in the dress that she had on. There was nothing else to be done: Maria took her seat in the carriage and was driven off, accompanied by the counsels and blessings of Anna Vlassievna.

Maria felt that our fate was about to be decided; her heart beat violently. In a few moments the carriage stopped at the gate of the palace. Maria descended the steps with trembling feet. The doors flew open before her. She traversed a large number of empty but magnificent rooms, guided by the lackey. At last, coming to a closed door, he informed her that she would be announced directly, and then left her by herself.

The thought of meeting the Empress face to face so terrified her, that she could scarcely stand upon her feet. In about a minute the door was opened, and she was ushered into the Empress's boudoir.

*Artist P.P. Sokolov, 19th century*

The Empress was seated at her toilette-table, surrounded by a number of Court ladies, who respectfully made way for Maria Ivanovna. The Empress turned round to her with an amiable smile, and Maria recognized in her the lady with whom she had spoken so freely a few minutes before. The Empress bade her approach, and said with a smile:

"I am glad that I am able to keep my word and grant your petition. Your business is arranged. I am convinced of the innocence of your lover. Here is a letter which you will give to your future father-in-law."

Maria took the letter with trembling hands and, bursting into tears, fell at the feet of the Empress, who raised her up and kissed her upon the forehead.

"I know that you are not rich," said she; "but I owe a debt to the daughter of Captain Mironoff. Do not be uneasy about the future. I will see to your welfare."

After having consoled the poor orphan in this way, the Empress allowed her to depart. Maria left the palace in the same carriage that had brought her thither. Anna Vlassievna, who was impatiently awaiting her return, overwhelmed her with questions, to which Maria returned very vague answers. Although dissatisfied with the weakness of her memory, Anna Vlassievna ascribed it to her provincial bashfulness, and magnanimously excused her. The same day Maria, without even desiring to glance at St. Petersburg, set out on her return journey.

\* \* \* \* \*

The memoirs of Peter Andreitch Grineff end here. But from a family tradition we learn that he was released from his imprisonment towards the end of the year 1774 by order of the Empress, and that he was present at the execution of Pougatcheff, who recognized him in the crowd and nodded to him with his head, which, a few moments afterwards, was shown lifeless and bleeding to the people. Shortly afterwards, Peter Andreitch and Maria Ivanovna were married. Their descendants still flourish in the government of Simbirsk. About thirty versts from — —, there is a village belonging to ten landholders. In the house of one of them, there may still be seen, framed and glazed, the autograph letter of Catherine II. It is addressed to the father of Peter Andreitch, and contains the justification of his son, and a tribute of praise to the heart and intellect of Captain Mironoff's daughter.

# Also available:

Alexander Pushkin. *Short Stories;*

Alexander Pushkin. *The Queen of Spades* (illustrations by Alexandre Benois);

Mikhail Lermontov. *A Hero of Our Time* (illustrated edition);

Leo Tolstoy. *Anna Karenina;*

William Shakespeare. *A Midsummer Night's Dream* (illustrations by Arthur Rackham);

*Stories from Hans Christian Andersen* (illustrations by W. Heath Robinson);

*Fairy Tales by Hans Andersen* (illustrations by Arthur Rackham);

*Fairy Tales of Charles Perrault* (illustrations by Walter Crane);

*Russian Fairy Tales* (illustrations by Ivan Bilibin);

Brothers Grimm. *Snow White* (illustrations by Franz Jüttner);

Hans Christian Andersen. *The Snow Queen* (illustrations by T. Pym);

Jeanne-Marie Le Prince de Beaumont. *Beauty and the Beast* (illustrations by Walter Crane).

*www.the-planet-books.com*